D0917045

ISABELLA

Isabella

Loretta Lynda Chase

Walker and Company
New York

First published in the United States of America in 1987 by the Walker
Publishing Company, Inc.

Published simultaneously in Canada by Thomas Allen & Son
Canada, Limited, Markham, Ontario.

Library of Congress Cataloging-in-Publication Data

Chase, Loretta Lynda, 1949-
   Isabella.

   I. Title.
PS3553.H334I8 1987   813'.54   87-10626
ISBN 0-8027-0975-3

Printed in the United States of America

10 9 8 7 6 5 4 3 2 1

1

"Disappeared!" the earl repeated, in a dangerously quiet voice. "What the devil do you mean, 'disappeared'? Seven-year-old girls don't just vanish."

The thin governess trembled. She had never heard *quite* that tone from her employer before, and would have preferred that he shout at her, for his suppressed fury was far more terrifying. Edward Trevelyan, seventh Earl of Hartleigh, was an extremely handsome man whose warm brown eyes had often set Miss Carter's forty-year-old heart aflutter. But at the moment, the brown eyes glittered down at her with barely contained rage. And though his voice was low, the temper he so carefully controlled showed in his long fingers, which now, as he questioned her, were angrily raking the thick dark curls at his forehead.

Stammering and tearful, Miss Carter tried to explain. She'd taken Lucy to the circulating library. They'd then decided to see if they could find a ribbon to match Lucy's newest and favourite dress. Miss Carter had stopped only a moment—to admire the cut of Lady Delmont's pelisse as that grand and rather scandalous personage entered the shop across the street. Apparently, the governess had let go of Lucy's hand. Not that she actually *remembered* letting go—she was so sure she hadn't—but she must have, for when she looked down beside her, Lucy was gone. She had searched all the nearby shops to no avail.

Turning away from the governess in disgust, Lord Hartleigh began snapping orders to his household. He dispatched a dozen servants to comb the streets, then called for his carriage, his hat, and his cane. When the door finally closed behind him, the remaining inhabitants commenced to whispering among themselves; all but Miss Carter, who, teary-eyed and red-faced, scurried to her room.

It served him right, he thought as the carriage made its way down the street. This was what came of being so hasty to hire a governess for his young ward. Yet Miss Carter had not seemed the least bit flighty—and she had come highly recommended. Even Aunt Clem had agreed with his choice of governess for Lucy. Well, actually, she had said, "I suppose she'll do—but *it* won't do, you know, Edward." Whatever "it" was. Clem had a tendency to fix you with her eye in that all-knowing way of hers and then utter cryptic pronouncements in the tone of a sybil.

Life certainly had changed when one must go to Aunt Clementina for advice, he thought ruefully. There was a time when he'd made his way across the Continent, close to Napoleon's forces, in search of information which would save English lives. But twice he'd endangered his own. He would be dead now if it hadn't been for Robert Warriner. Instead, it was Robert who was gone. News of his death had been delivered a month ago by the housekeeper's husband, along with a letter . . . and a seven-year-old girl.

The letter was short, and he had read it often enough to know it by heart, especially the closing lines:

> *It is rather a great favor I ask, my friend. But the doctors have no hope for me, and Lucy will be left alone in the world. Our housekeeper and her husband have offered to take her in, but they are hard-pressed to care for themselves, and I cannot place such a burden on them. For old times' sake, then, will you watch over my daughter as though she were your own?*

Watch over her. And now the child was lost in the middle of a busy and dangerous city. Oh, Robert, forgive me, he thought.

"Mademoiselle Latham, you must trust me. I do not cut the gowns simply *à la mode*. I cut *pour la femme*. But see, how can you judge?" Nudging her recalcitrant customer along to the dressing room, Madame Vernisse continued in that sing-song of hers. "First you must try it on, and then we shall see what we shall see."

Although she obediently followed the modiste into the dressing room, everything within Isabella cried out for escape, and she had the mad urge to dash back out of the room, the shop, and London altogether. Back to Westford and the home she and her widowed mother had made with quiet, sensible Uncle Henry Latham. Life in Westford might be dull at times, and Aunt Pamela's social climbing a source of embarrassment, but there at least Isabella was not the object of constant scrutiny and speculation. Why, Lady Delmont had stared at her quite rudely, and for no other reason than that Isabella was Maria Latham's daughter. Well, let her stare. Mama may have disgusted her family by marrying Matthew Latham—a mere cit—but she was Viscount Belcomb's sister, nonetheless. And unlike her brother Thomas, Maria Latham was quite plump in the pockct. Isabella raised her chin just a little as Madame Vernisse slipped the blue silk gown over her head. And when the modiste stepped back with a little smile to admire her handiwork, Miss Latham bravely looked into the mirror.

It was lovely. It was also a trifle . . . shocking. "Madame Vernisse, are you certain . . . ?" She motioned vaguely toward her bosom, an alarming expanse of which was in public view.

"It is perfection on you," the modiste replied. "Of course the fashion is much more *décolleté* than this—but as I tell you, I do not cut just for the fashion; I cut also for the *femme*."

It was amazing what a new frock could do. The elegantly cut gown clung to her slim figure, calling attention to previously well-concealed curves. The rich blue deepened the blue of her eyes and made her complexion seem creamily luminous. Even her dingy blonde hair had taken on a golden luster. She looked, in fact, almost *pretty*. Not that it signified how she looked. After all, this was her two cousins' first Season. Isabella need only look well enough to appear with them in public.

Thinking of the coming months, Isabella suddenly felt weary. She would have much preferred to stay quietly in the country with Uncle Henry and Aunt Pamela Latham, her late father's brother and his wife. It was, as Mama had said, a great bore to go where one was not welcome. But Aunt Pamela wanted her eldest daughter, Isabella's cousin Alicia, to have a London Season; it was hoped the girl would find herself a titled husband. And so Mama had been persuaded to write to her estranged brother, the viscount, with a simple proposal: The Lathams would be pleased to finance a Season for the viscount's daughter, Veronica Belcomb, if, in return, Alicia Latham was also provided entrée into Society. It was a bitter pill for the Belcombs to swallow, but they had little choice, as Aunt Pamela well knew. "Barely a feather to fly with," she'd said. "Veronica's dowry is nothing to speak of—and what good is even that, I ask you, when they can't afford a Season for her?"

The blue gown was gently removed, and an emerald-green gown took its place, to be in turn replaced by a series of walking dresses, and a deep forest-green riding habit.

"You see?" said Madame Vernisse. "The colours of the sea, and of the cool forest. And so your hair glows and your eyes sparkle. Was I not correct?"

Isabella nodded agreement, but her mind was on her family and its problems. And when her ever-restless abigail, Polly, offered to run some errands while the fittings continued, Isabella dismissed her with an absent nod.

To soften the blow to the Belcomb pride, Maria Latham had proposed herself as chaperone. This would save Lady Belcomb the embarrassment of being seen too much in public with a girl whose father was engaged in *trade*. And,

4

of course, it would save her ladyship the expense of a new wardrobe—for it was one thing to take advantage of her only chance to see her daughter properly launched; it was quite another to be beholden to the Lathams for the very clothes on her own back. And so the offer was accepted, and Lady Belcomb had little to do but tolerate the three Lathams under her roof and smooth the way for her sister-in-law—whom society had not seen in twenty-seven years. The rest would be up to Maria.

It was unfortunate that Mama and Uncle Henry had both insisted on Isabella's coming to London as well. Of course, it was too much to expect her languid parent to be in constant attendance on a pair of "tiresomely energetic schoolroom misses," even though she had proposed herself as nominally their chaperone. The real task would fall to Isabella. And after all, they were under tremendous obligation to Uncle Henry, for had he not welcomed them into his home after Papa died, and helped them rebuild the fortune Matt Latham had speculated away? She came back to the present with a jolt when she heard the modiste's voice at her ear.

"So, mam'selle, I think we have done well for today. And by the end of the week, we shall have the others ready as well. *Bon.* It is a good day's work, I think." Nodding approval at her own artistry, Madame Vernisse was so pleased with herself that she even condescended to help Isabella back into her somber brown frock, although the modiste did frown as she fastened up the back and tactfully suggested that it be given—as soon as possible—to Polly. And then she hustled out of the dressing room, and promptly began scolding her assistants, who weren't looking busy enough to suit her.

Several pins had come loose from Isabella's hair, and she stopped to make repairs before leaving the dressing room. As she glanced in the mirror, she was a little disappointed to see a dowdy spinster again, and sighed. A tiny sigh echoed it, and she looked around quickly. No one in the room but herself. Then she heard it again. It seemed to be coming from a pile of discarded lining fabric that had fallen into a corner. Evidently it had been a busy day for the modiste; normally, the shop was scrupulously tidy.

Cautiously, Isabella stepped toward the fabric. It moved slightly, and emitted a whimper. As she moved closer, she saw a tiny hand clutching a red ribbon. She lifted a corner of the fabric to find a little girl, asleep. As Isabella gently smoothed the tousled brown curls away from her face, the child, who had somehow managed to sleep through the earlier chatter in the dressing room, awoke to the caress. "Mama?" she whispered. Then, when she realized that this was a stranger, the tears welled up in her eyes. "She's gone away," she told Isabella, and began sobbing as though her heart would break.

When Madame Vernisse reentered the dressing room to see what had become of her latest client, she was shocked to find that young lady seated on the floor, cradling a little girl in her arms.

"And so your name is Lucy, is it?" Isabella inquired, some minutes later, after the child had been comforted and her tears bribed away with sweets. "Is that all of your name?"

"Lucy Warriner," the girl answered.

"Oh, blessed heavens. It is Milord 'artleigh's ward," cried Madame Vernisse. "They will be frantic for her. I must send someone *immédiatement*. Michelle! Michelle! Where is that girl when you want her? Not here. Never here. Where does she go, I ask?"

"Polly will be back in a moment," Isabella replied, calmly. "We'll send her." Turning back to Lucy, she asked, "And how did you get lost in the dressing room?"

"Oh, I didn't get lost," the child replied. "I excaped."

"What did you escape from?"

"That lady. Miss Carter. My govermiss."

Suppressing a smile, Isabella continued, "I should think Miss Carter would be worried sick about you, Lucy. Don't

6

you know it's wrong to escape from your governess? She's there to take care of you."

"Papa took care of me. He didn't get a govermiss. Even after Mama went to heaven, he took care of me himself. I don't need a govermiss. But I miss my Papa." As tears threatened again, Isabella gave up her questioning and offered hugs instead.

When another quarter hour had passed and Polly had not yet returned, Isabella determined—despite Madame Vernisse's vociferous Gallic protests—to escort the child back to the earl's house herself. So it was that she emerged from the mantua-maker's shop with Lucy's hand in hers and nearly collided with a very tall, very well-dressed, and very angry gentleman.

"I beg your—" he began irritatedly. His eye then fell upon Lucy, who was attempting to hide in Isabella's skirts. "Lucy! What is this?" He glared down at Isabella from his more than six-foot height. "That child is my ward, miss," he growled. "I assume you have some explanation."

Stunned by this unexpected rudeness, and not a little cowed by his size, Isabella stared, speechless, at him. She felt Lucy's grip on her hand tighten. This was the girl's guardian? The poor child was terrified of him.

"Perhaps you would be kind enough to release her," Lord Hartleigh continued, reaching for Lucy's free hand. Lucy, however, backed off.

At this Isabella found her tongue. "I will be happy to—if in fact you are her guardian, and if you would calm yourself. You're frightening her."

Hearing the commotion, Madame Vernisse hurried to the entrance. "Ah, Milord 'artleigh. You have arrived at the *bon moment*. We have found your ward!" she cried triumphantly.

"So I see," he snapped. "Then perhaps you would be kind enough to tell your assistant to let me take the girl home."

Madame Vernisse looked from one to the other in bewilderment. "But Milord—"

"Never mind," said Isabella. She was shaking with anger, but endeavoured to control her voice as she bent to speak to the little girl. "Now, Lucy, your guardian is here to take you back home."

"I don't want to," Lucy replied. "I excaped."

"Yes, and you have worried Lord Hartleigh terribly. You see? He is so distraught that he forgets his manners and blusters at ladies." This last caused the earl's ears to redden, but he held his tongue, sensing that he was at a disadvantage. "Now if you go nicely with him, he'll feel better and will not shout at the servants when you get home."

"You come, too," Lucy begged. "You can be my mama."

"No, dear. I must go back to my own family, or they'll worry about me, too."

"Then take me with you," the child persisted.

"No, dear. You must go back with your guardian. You don't want to worry him anymore, do you? Or hurt his feelings?"

The notion of this giant's having tender feelings which could be hurt was a bit overwhelming for the child, but she shook her head obediently.

Isabella stood up again. Reluctantly, the little hand slipped from her own, the brown curls emerged from their hiding place, and Lucy allowed her guardian to take her hand. "I'm sorry I worried you, Uncle Edward," she told him contritely. "I'm ready to go home now." As they began to walk to his carriage, she turned back briefly, to offer Isabella one sad little wave good-bye.

The missing Polly reappeared in time to see the earl lift Lucy into the carriage and then climb in himself. "Oh, miss," she gasped. "Do you see who that is?"

"Yes. It is Lord Hartleigh. And it is time we went home."

"A spy, you know, miss," Polly went on, hurrying to keep up with her mistress, who was clearly in a tizzy about something. "They say he was a spy against those wicked Frenchies. And they caught him, miss, you know, and threw him in prison, and he nearly died of the fever there, but he got away from them. And then came back half-dead. Laid up for months, he was. And all for his country. He's a real hero—as much as My Lord Wellington—but it's a secret, you know." She sighed. "Lor', such a handsome man. The shoulders on him—did you notice, miss?"

"Handsome is as handsome does," snapped her mistress. "Do hurry. I promised to be home for nuncheon."

Lord Hartleigh had ample time to consider his behaviour during the silent ride home. After all, one could not expect Lucy to speak. She was always sad and withdrawn, and speaking to her only made her sadder and more withdrawn. It was only at Aunt Clem's that the child had shown any sign of animation. But Lucy had not been the least shy with that strange woman at the dressmaker's. Good heavens, she'd even asked her to be her mama! As he recalled the scene, he was filled with self-loathing. What an overbearing bully he must have looked!

His behaviour that day had been abominable: Cold and impatient with Miss Carter, he had gone on to make a complete ass of himself at the modiste's. But he had been turned inside out by worry—and guilt. That hour he'd spent searching the shops had seemed like months. Robert had trusted his child to him. And after less than a month, this trusted guardian had proceeded to misplace her. I take better care of my horses, the earl thought miserably.

He glanced again at Lucy. She was the image of her father, with her hazel eyes and curling brown hair, but she had none of his spirit. Not that her recent losses weren't enough to stifle the spirit of even the liveliest child. Pity for her welled up in him, and he felt again the same frustration he'd felt for weeks: He could not make her happy. Why had she run away? And what was so appealing about this dowdy young woman that Lucy wanted to go away and live with her?

Of course, that fair-haired young woman had *not* been the dressmaker's assistant; he should have known it as soon as she opened her mouth. He'd seen her somewhere before . . . at one of those dreary affairs to which Aunt Clem was forever sending him in search of a suitable wife? Or had it been somewhere else? No matter. He should have known by her dignity and poise that she was a lady. But he'd been too distraught to think clearly. He smiled ruefully. Distraught and blustering. Just as the young lady had explained so patiently to Lucy. He had simply reacted—out of fear for Lucy's safety and, it must be admitted, hurt pride. It was not agreeable for a man who'd taken responsibility for the safety of whole armies to discover that he could not adequately oversee the care of one little girl. Nor was it agreeable to see the way the child had clung to that woman, or the reluctance with which she had come to him.

But it was to be expected, was it not? Lucy wanted a mama; so badly that she would pick up strange women on the street. Well, if a mama was what was required, he would supply one. It was not pleasant to think of, but when before had he shunned a dangerous mission?

Dangerous. That was it. The woman he'd seen early the other morning, dashing across the meadow on that spirited brown mare. Good God! Lord Belcomb's niece.

Looking up timidly, Lucy saw that her guardian's face was turning red. Fearful of a scolding, she shrank farther into her corner.

2

"Do my eyes deceive me, Freddie? Or has a new face actually entered this redoubt of redundancy, this mansion of monotony?"

Young Lord Tuttlehope looked toward the doorway where Lord and Lady Belcomb had just entered, accompanied by a nondescript blonde young woman in a modish blue gown. Blinking away his friend's literary flourishes, he responded to the few words he understood. "Matt Latham's daughter. Belcomb's niece. Got a few thousand a year."

Basil Trevelyan lifted an eyebrow. "How few?"

"Ten or twenty. Maybe more. Matt blew up most of what he had in one scheme or another. But Henry took them in hand. Clever man, Henry. Shrewd investor."

Basil's interest increased. His topaz eyes half-closed in apparent boredom, he nonetheless watched the trio make their way through the room until they settled in a corner with Lady Stirewell and her daughter.

"Indeed. Charming girl, don't you think?"

Freddie blinked uncomprehendingly at his friend. The two had been at Oxford together and maintained a friendship ever since; yet it may safely be supposed that Lord Tuttlehope understood only a fraction of what his companion said or did. However, he made up for his slow wit with a strong loyalty. "Barely met the girl myself," he replied. "Introduced at the Fordhulls' dinner. Sat the other end of the table. Never said a word. Don't blame her. Meal was abominable. Fordhulls never could keep a good cook."

"My dear Freddie," Basil drawled, still watching the young woman, who had embarked upon a lively conversation with the youngest Stirewell daughter, "it does not require an intimate relationship to ascertain that a young woman with an income of more than ten or twenty thousand a year must perforce be charming. And to those already considerable charms, one must add the mystique of scandal. Didn't her mother up and run off a week after her come-out?"

"Heard something about it. Never said whom she'd run off with. Six months later sends word she's married the merchant—and breeding," Freddie added with a blush.

"I thought Belcomb had washed his hands of his regrettable sister and her more regrettable spouse and offspring. Or hath ready blunt the power to soothe even the savage Belcomb beast?"

His speech earning him two blinks, Basil translated, "Is his lordship so sadly out of pocket that he's reconciled with his sister?"

The light of comprehension dawned in Lord Tuttlehope's eyes. "Thought you knew," he responded. "Bet at White's he'd be down to cook and butler by the end of the Season. Staff got restless—hadn't paid 'em in months. Then the Lathams turned up."

"I see." And certainly he did. No stranger to creditors himself, Basil easily understood the viscount's recent willingness to overlook his sister's unfortunate commercial attachment. Though he was barely thirty years old, Basil Trevelyan had managed to run up debts enough to wipe out a small country. Until two years ago, he'd relied on his uncle—then earl of Hartleigh—to rescue him from his creditors. But those halcyon days were at an end. Edward Trevelyan, his cousin, was the new Earl of Hartleigh and had made it clear, not long after assuming the title, that there would be no further support from that quarter.

Basil had remained optimistic. Edward, after all, regularly engaged in extremely risky intelligence missions abroad, and one could reasonably expect him to be killed off one fine day soon—and, of course, to leave title and fortune to his more deserving cousin. Disappointingly, upon his father's death Edward haad dutifully ceased risking his life on England's behalf, and had taken up his responsibilities as a Peer of the Realm.

"Not in the petticoat line myself, you know," Freddie remarked, "but she ain't much to look at. And past her prime. Closer to thirty than not."

His friend appeared, at first, not to hear him. Basil's attention was still fixed on the viscount's party. It was only after Lady Belcomb finally let her glance stray in his direction that he turned back to his companion, picking up the conversation as though several empty minutes had not passed.

"Yes, it is rather sad, Freddie, how the uncharming poor girls look like Aphrodite and the charming rich ones like Medusa."

Lord Tuttlehope, whose own attention had drifted longingly toward the refreshment room, recalled himself with a blink. After mentally reviewing the stables of his acquaintance and recollecting no horses which went by these names, he contented himself with what he believed was a knowing look. "Always the way, Basil, don't you know?"

"And I must marry a Medusa. It isn't fair, Freddie. Just consider my thoughtless cousin Edward. Title, fortune, thirty-five years old, still a bachelor. Should he die, I inherit all. But *will* he show a little family feeling and get on with it? No. Did he have the grace to pass on three years ago, when the surgeons, quite intelligently, all shook their heads and walked away? No. These risky missions of his have never been quite risky enough."

"A demmed shame, Trev. Never needed the money either. Demmed unfair."

Basil smiled appreciatively at his friend's loyal sympathy. "And as if that weren't exasperating enough, along comes the orphan to help spend his money before I get to it. And

13

to ice the cake, I now hear from Aunt Clem that he's thinking to set up his own nursery."

"Demmed shame," muttered his friend.

"Ah, but we must live in hope, my friend. Hope of, say, Miss Latham. Not unreasonably high an aspiration. Perhaps this once the Fates will look down on me favourably. At least she doesn't look like a cit—although she obviously doesn't take after her mother. Aunt Clem said Maria Belcomb was a beauty—and there was something odd in the story . . . oh well." Basil shrugged and turned his attention once more to the pale young lady in blue. Seeing that the viscount had abandoned his charges for the card room, he straightened and, lifting his chin, imagined himself a Bourbon about to be led to the guillotine. "Come, Freddie. You know Lady Belcomb. I wish to be introduced to her niece."

Miss Stirewell having been swept away by her mother to gladden the eyes and hearts of the unmarried gentlemen present (and, possibly, to avoid the two ne'er-do-wells who seemd to be moving in their direction), Isabella Latham tried to appear interested as her aunt condescended to identify the Duchess of Chilworth's guests. Her grace's entertainments were famous, her invitations desperately sought and savagely fought for, with the result that anyone of the ton worth knowing was bound to be there, barring mortal illness. "Even the Earl of Hartleigh," Lady Belcomb added. "For I understand he's given up those foreign affairs and is finally settling down."

Isabella's cheeks grew pink at the mention of the name. Though a week had passed since that scene at the dressmaker's shop, she still had not fully recovered her equanimity. True, the earl had called the day after the contretemps to make a very proper, though cool, apology—to which she had responded equally coolly and properly. Lady Belcomb had absented herself for a moment (to arrange for Veronica's "accidental" appearance), and Mama, as usual, was resting. Thus none of the family had been privy to their conversation. However, the footman who stood at the door guarding her reputation had heard every syllable, and Isabella wondered what exaggerated form the drama would have taken by the time it reached her aunt's ears.

"Indeed," that lady continued, "it was most astonishing, his coming to call. But he *is* rumoured to be seeking a wife. And Veronica was looking well Tuesday, was she not?"

"She is always lovely, Aunt," Isabella replied. She had not missed the increased warmth in the earl's manner when Veronica entered the room. Nor, when those haughty brown eyes had been turned upon herself, had she failed to notice how he'd sized her up, appraising her head to toe and, in seconds, tallying her value at zero. Not that it mattered. It was her cousin's Season to shine. At the advanced age of twenty-six, Isabella Latham need not trouble her head with the appraisals of bored Corinthians.

"It is a pity their come-out had to be put off so late," Isabella continued, forcing the handsome and haughty earl from her mind. "For Alicia and Veronica might have been here to enjoy this with us."

"Well, well. Alicia could not be presented to society in a wardrobe made by the village scamstress."

"That is true, Aunt."

"And after all," Lady Belcomb went on, not noticing the irony of her niece's tone, "there will be festivities enough. Although this is quite a brilliant assembly—did you notice Lady Delmont's emeralds? I was not aware her husband . . . but then, never mind." Reluctantly, she turned from contemplation of the jewels on Lady Delmont's bosom. "Veronica will have plenty of time to shine, along with your other little cousin. It is but two weeks until their little *fête.*"

Her niece looked down to hide the smile quivering on her lips. While the viscountess had accepted the exigencies of fate and graciously agreed to oversee preparations for the come-out ball, she was compelled to reduce the situation to diminutives. Thus the come-out for Veronica and Alicia, costing the Lathams many hundreds of pounds, was a "little" party, and Alicia herself, though three inches taller than Lady Belcomb, a "countrified little thing."

"That reminds me; we must be certain Lord Hartleigh has been sent an invitation. It would be mortifying, after his thoughtful visit, to discover he had not been included."

Isabella, who had, purely on her cousins' account, resisted the temptation to hurl said invitation into the fire, assured her aunt that all was well. With the coming ball, Lady Belcomb's responsibilities would cease, according to the agreement. It would then be up to Isabella to accompany her cousins on their debutante rounds, for Mama was bound to be too tired, or too bored. Idly, Isabella wondered where she would fit in. Would she be required to sit with the rest of the gossiping duennas and attempt to converse with them? Did chaperones dance? The music had just begun, and Isabella looked down to see her white satin slippers tapping in time, as though they had nothing to do with respectable chaperones. Were chaperones allowed to tap their toes to the music? Smiling at the thought, she looked up to meet a pair of glittering topaz eyes gazing down at her.

"Lady Belcomb, Miss Latham, may I present Mr Basil Trevelyan," Lord Tuttlehope announced, with the air of one introducing Prinny himself. And she should count herself lucky, Freddie thought. Mousy old thing for Basil to be leg-shackled to, poor chap, with all his romantic poetical nonsense.

But Mr Trevelyan was looking at the possible answer to his prayers. Hadn't Aunt Clem warned him that few parents would care to put their daughters' fortunes in his hands? "Even I should not," she warned him, "though I do believe you'll outgrow it in time."

The Lathams, however, might be willing to trade some thousands of pounds to improve their position in society. Thus he had determined to find the unprepossessing Miss Latham charming, and to charm her in turn. After suitably flattering Lady Belcomb and hinting at the eagerness with which her daughter's entry into society was awaited, he left her to Freddie, and turned those strange amber cat eyes back to Isabella. "I understand, Miss Latham, that you are new to London."

"Quite new—unless you count my first visit, at the age of five."

"Ah, you were cruel to abandon us. Hard-hearted even at such a tender age. But we must be thankful that you have relented toward us at last, and must endeavour to correct your previously poor opinion."

Perhaps it was the penetrating gaze which unsettled her, as she conjured up the image of a five-year-old *femme fatale*. At any rate, her careful poise cracked for a moment, and laughter escaped. It was a low, husky laughter; a haunting, inviting sound, completely out of place in this large public gathering.

Her aunt cast a puzzled glance in her direction. Was Isabella flirting with Trevelyan? Lady Belcomb would have wagered half her stable (were it still hers to wager) that her niece had no more knowledge of flirtation that she had of flying. No matter. Trevelyan's expensive tastes were well known, and he was decidedly an unsuitable match for Veronica. This niece (and any of her Latham cousins, in the bargain) was welcome to him; at least *his* family was unexceptionable. That settled, the viscountess resumed her debate with Lord Tuttlehope over the merits of certain horses of their acquaintance.

For his part, Basil was pleasantly surprised: The Answer to His Prayers had a mind not quite so dull as her face. As he stared, puzzling, at her, Isabella, imagining that she had committed some sort of indiscretion by laughing at her interlocutor's extravagant comments, blushed. She did not know that the combination of heightened color and sparkling blue eyes transformed her face from nothing remarkable into something which, in a quiet way, was rather lovely. Nor did she have any inkling of why her laughter caused people to stare.

Indeed, she would have reddened to her fingertips had she known the thoughts it conjured up in the tawny-haired young man with the unsettling eyes. Basil found himself wondering what it would be like to hear that laughter rather closer to his ear, in more intimate circumstances. The thought cheered him enormously, as he studied her with increased enthusiasm—and curiosity. "Miss Latham," he continued, his voice dropping almost to a whisper, "I declare you are cruel still. Here am I so deadly serious, so monstrous earnest, and I succeed only in throwing you into fits of laughter. Perhaps, though, you suspect I am attempting to turn your head with flattery. Perhaps for some nefarious purpose?"

This time she controlled herself, and only a twitching at the corner of her mouth hinted at laughter. "I suspect," she replied, "only that you are talking arrant nonsense and that you do so to amuse yourself. Is London life so dull, then?"

"Dreary as an Irish bog—until now," he whispered, bending closer. Then, noticing that Lady Belcomb's attention had drifted back to them, he straightened and, in louder tones, requested the honour of a dance.

Stunned by the suggestiveness of his tone, Isabella could not think how to refuse him politely. She knew the relatively straightforward methods of business, but society and its ways were painfully indirect and convoluted. Certainly she could not tell him that he made her uncomfortable. There was something so . . . *feline* about him: the tawny hair and those strange amber eyes that slanted upward like a cat's. Eyes that were watchful, penetrating, even under their bored, sleepy lids.

"I promise I shan't bite," he said with a smile, leading her to the dancing area. "Although the ton may, if you have not been approved to waltz."

Although she privately felt that, considering her advanced age, such approval was rather irrelevant, Isabella assured him that she had been deemed worthy by the Almack's patronesses. And then she wished she had not, for while she had been taught, along with her cousins, to waltz, it had never before struck her as so perilous an enterprise. Dancing so close to him, her hand on his shoulder, she realised with some shock that he was more powerfully built than he seemed. He was only a few inches taller than herself, and slender, yet he had a supple strength which belied his slight appearance. The hand at her back was uncomfortably warm, despite his gloves, and it pressed her closer than seemed entirely necessary.

Apparently unaware of his partner's unease, Basil made light conversation (interspersed with generous doses of flattery), interrogating her about the sights she had seen thus far and her impressions of the city and its people. He was chagrined to learn that she had not yet been to Hyde Park, had not visited the Tower or the Mansion House or the Guildhall. *She* was chagrined to learn it was his intention to correct these oversights, personally. It was useless trying to explain that in attending to her two young cousins, she would have precious little time for sightseeing. "We'll take the little girls along with us, Miss Latham" was his rejoinder.

"They are not precisely little. . . ." she began uncomfortably.

"I daresay not. Nor am I—precisely—concerned with improving upon their education. I am not acting from purely altruistic motives; quite the contrary. But you see, society requires that we observe certain proprieties, and I believe I should prefer the superfluous company of your cousins to that of disapproving aunts."

Again she blushed. His tone seemed to lace every sentence with innuendo. "Mr Trevelyan," she protested, "I wish you would recall that I am a mere naïve from the country and haven't the faintest notion what you are about. Did I somehow give you the impression that I am in the habit of roaming about strange cities in the company of strange men?"

The music stopped.

"I rather wish that you were," he murmured as he released her. "But at any rate, I would hope to become less of a stranger."

"So you have made abundantly clear. Are all London gentlemen as forward as you?" she asked as he escorted her back to her aunt.

"I daresay not. But I am rather a dreadful young man, as Aunt Clem is sure to tell you." He indicated a large woman of about sixty, who had just joined Lady Belcomb. Dressed in mauve, and wearing an ornate turban which made her appear to tower over the rest of the guests, the Countess Bertram was an awesome sight. Her height, her grand bearing, the slightly hawkish cast of her nose, all put one in mind of a warrior goddess. Indeed, she seemed to lack only armour and shield to complete the picture.

"Lady Bertram," said the viscountess, "I do not believe you have met my niece, Isabella Latham."

Both ladies pronouncing themselves delighted, Lady Bertram turned her sharp brown eyes to Basil. "So the prodigal returns," she drawled. "Miss Latham, I see you have already had the dubious honor of meeting my disreputable nephew."

"Aunt Clem! How very naughty of you. And here I have gone to heaps of trouble to present myself to these ladies in the most respectable light possible."

"A physical impossibility," the lady retorted. "I must warn you against him, Miss Latham. This disrespectful scapegrace has not deigned to call on his aunt in three weeks. And a woman of my age has not many weeks to waste." In punctuation, she tapped his arm with her fan and sat down.

"I am sure Mr Trevelyan cannot be as dreadful as you say," Lady Belcomb felt compelled to remark, though she firmly believed otherwise.

"Honourable chap, must say," added Lord Tuttlehope.

"And what do *you* say, Miss Latham? Or has he exercised his wicked charm upon you too?"

It occurred to Isabella that Lady Bertram had a pretty fair knowledge of her nephew—and possibly of the perils of dancing with him. As she turned to that lady to respond, she thought she glimpsed something sympathetic in the face beneath the mauve turban.

"I am afraid he has," Isabella answered. "But as he has just this moment himself assured me that he is perfectly dreadful, and as blood is thicker than water, I must submit to family opinion."

"Isabella!" her aunt exclaimed in disapproval. But Lady Bertram waved her away much as she would an annoying insect.

"Intelligent gel, Lady Belcomb. There's more sense in her than in both my nephews combined. Speaking of which, here comes the other one, to honour us with his company."

The turban nodded in the direction of Lord Hartleigh, who was disconcerted to find five sets of eyes fixed upon him. One pair in particular, sparkling like a matched set of aquamarines, unnerved him. His demeanour belied his discomfort, however, and only his aunt noted the minute crack in the calm social mask. He greeted the two elder women warmly, bowed courteously to Isabella, and coolly acknowledged his cousin and the young baron.

The next quarter hour was not the most agreeable of his life. Lord Hartleigh had intended only to stop for a minute, primarily to greet his aunt, but upon discovering that Basil had planted himself among the party and refused to depart, the earl stubbornly stood his ground. He was not certain why. Basil always irritated him, and he knew his own continued existence was an irritation to Basil. In addition, he was uneasy attempting to make conversation with Miss Latham, who had seen him at his worst—he, the Earl of Hartleigh, known for his unerring courtesy.

But there was Basil, hovering over the young lady like one of those jungle cats hovering over its prey. Nonsense. His mind was working like some silly romance. But somehow she had aroused the earl's protective instincts, and he hesitated to leave her with no sentinel in attendance but his unpredictable aunt, since it was clear that Lady Belcomb either didn't know or didn't care that Basil was a fortune hunter.

Why he should concern himself, he didn't know. All he knew was that he wanted his cousin as far away from Miss Latham as possible. And since Basil appeared to have no intention of budging, Lord Hartleigh determined to remove the young lady. Therefore, to both their surprise, he asked her to dance.

Although the earl had done nothing to endear himself to her, she accepted his offer with an enormous sense of relief, as a means of escaping his cousin's overpowering presence. She was dismayed to find herself attracted to the . . . creature. Never in her life had she been so showered with poetic compliments, and she had begun to think that his "wicked charm" might indeed turn her head, for there was something so tempting about wickedness, wasn't there? Rakish young men were rather like forbidden sweets: You knew they weren't good for you and you'd suffer for trying them, but they were so very . . . seductive. What a monstrous improper train of thought! Gladly, she put it aside as Lord Hartleigh's arm encircled her waist.

This, too, was a waltz, but her response to this cousin was very different. Wasn't it odd that the one who had responded so warmly to her had frightened her, while this one, towering over her, who had insulted her and then dismissed her with cool arrogance, did not intimidate her in the least?

They were alike in some ways. There was a family resemblance in the high cheekbones, the clear strong angles of the face, the long aristocratic nose. But there was nothing feline about Lord Hartleigh. His deep brown eyes, though betraying no emotion, appeared to gaze frankly at the world. His was not the catlike grace of his cousin but, instead, the assertive grace of the athlete. And the strong arm around her waist made her feel protected, rather than threatened.

Stiffly, they conversed about the weather, the temperature of the room, the attractive decorations. Then, quite abruptly (and to his own surprise), the earl changed the subject. "Miss Latham," he observed, "I do believe we got off on the wrong foot." Her startled eyes met his for a second, then looked away—into his neckcloth. However had he managed the perfect creases of that complicated arrangement? "I was rude to you once," he went on, "and compounded it with an equally rude apology. May we close the curtain on that unfortunate scene and begin fresh? My behaviour was inexcusable, but I ask that you dismiss it—as an unaccountable aberration."

"You were concerned about your ward," she replied.

"That is no excuse—"

"It is forgotten," she interrupted, smiling up at him.

It was Lord Hartleigh's turn to feel relieved, but his feelings were complicated by a new sensation: As he watched her face change with that smile, he felt a rather uncomfortable constriction in the general vicinity of his chest. Her eyes had softened to a deeper, smokier blue, and the curve of her lips was deliciously sensual. Several mute seconds passed as he gazed down into this suddenly very appealing face; seconds in which some unexpected notions drifted into his head. But he managed to recall himself in time. Clearing his throat, he told her that she was very . . . *kind*.

"And how *is* Lucy?" she asked.

This led to a discussion of various domestic details which Hartleigh had never previously considered. His bewilderment was plain—though he seemed to speak of it with humour—and when he quoted Aunt Clem's declaration that "the poor child was bored to tears in that stuffy house," Isabella laughed. The notion of this handsome, sophisticated, perfectly mannered, perfectly dressed Peer rendered helpless by a seven-year-old was highly diverting. As soon as she had shown her amusement, however, she regretted it; he would not like to be laughed at. Several couples dancing nearby were staring at them, and her face flushed crimson.

"I beg your pardon, Lord Hartleigh," she apologised hastily. "I am not used to being in such fine company, and fear I have a case of the nervous giggles."

He barely heard her, having become preoccupied with the constriction that was making it so difficult to breathe. Surely that deliciously wicked sound had not come from *her*. A host of even odder notions crowded into his brain, and he was very hard put to squash them. At length he managed to mutter something about a "perfectly absurd situation," and the dance, mercifully, ended.

It was a greatly unsettled Earl of Hartleigh who returned to his home that evening. He had gone to Lady Chilworth's ball specifically for the purpose of finding a mama for Lucy. Aunt Clem had provided a list of eligible females, and he had attempted to dance with all of them. He was determined to perceive this search for a mama as a mission: dangerous, yes, but critical to his ward's well-being. And to some extent he had begun to feel a bit of the excitement his political missions had engendered. But tonight he found himself unable to attend to his partners' conversation. He would gaze into their faces, expecting that each in turn would trigger some special response, and then would feel unaccountably irritated that they did not. He heard other laughter, and it irked him. Thus, as he guided one after another eligible young beauty through one after another dance, his attention would stray to a not-especially-pretty young lady in blue. And it was most provoking that Basil did not leave her side the entire evening.

3

The following day, the Belcomb home, already in chaos with preparations for the ball, was further disrupted by a parade of elegant gentlemen. Word of Isabella's material charms had long since made the rounds, but the attentions of the Trevelyan cousins the night before had considerably raised her market value among impoverished younger sons. Her dance card had rapidly filled from the moment that her dance with Lord Hartleigh ended. Basil, who had hoped for a relatively clear field, had not been pleased, but contented himself with hovering nearby and ingratiating himself with her aunt.

Today, then, all those who'd been privileged to dance with her made their courtesy calls. Lady Belcomb was not altogether happy at first with Isabella's sudden popularity, for it would appear to decrease her own daughters' prospects proportionately. But then, as she noted that the callers—*with one unfortunate exception*—were of straitened financial circumstances, her equanimity was restored, and she greeted them, if not graciously, then at least with forbearance. Unfortunately for the earlier callers, she was the only one to greet them. Isabella's customary morning ride (an exercise she took primarily to escape the quarrelling servants) had been later than usual, and she hadn't yet changed. Thus, Lord Hartleigh, among the early arrivals—and the *one unfortunate exception*—was disappointed.

Fortune smiled on Basil, however. He arrived shortly after Isabella joined her aunt. All the other callers had left or were compelled to leave (the proper half hour having expired), and he and Freddie had the field to themselves. Having paid his courteous compliments to Lady Belcomb, Basil had just settled himself comfortably to flattering an uncomfortable Isabella when there was a tumult at the door.

Sounds of merriment drifted into the room, to be followed in another moment by Alicia Latham, who was trailed by an anxious abigail. Laughingly, the girl scolded her maid. "No, no, Mary. It is quite all right. We can see to that later, but first I must see Isabella—" She stopped short as she saw the two gentlemen in the room.

Lord Tuttlehope, who had been detailing the merits of a pair of greys seen the previous day at Tattersall's, stopped midsentence, and his jaw dropped at the vision before him.

Alicia's windblown straw-coloured curls tumbled recklessly from her bonnet. Her green eyes sparkled; her cherry-pink lips were moist and parted slightly in surprise. Blushing at the sight of the two elegant gentlemen, she was, all in all, so pretty and innocent and fresh that even the most jaded rakehell could not fail to be charmed.

But where women were concerned, Lord Tuttlehope could hardly be termed *jaded.* An excruciating shyness had resulted in a virtually complete ignorance of the other sex. But, shy as he was, he couldn't help staring. The green eyes met his for a moment, then quickly lowered in confusion. In that moment, his heart gave a great leap and abandoned him.

Basil quickly rose and bowed, then found he had to nudge his friend to attention. After a second's paralysis, Lord Tuttlehope remembered what his limbs were expected to do.

"I'm so sorry. I didn't know—oh dear," Alicia stammered.

"Don't be silly, love," her cousin replied as she rose from her seat to lead the hesitating girl into the room. "You've finished your shopping early, I see."

"Yes. Oh dear. I did not mean. . . ." She glanced quickly at the gentlemen and blushed again.

Since Lady Belcomb simply sat there gazing at the girl with disapproval, Isabella made the introductions. Basil pronounced himself charmed, Lord Tuttlehope stammered something incomprehensible, and Isabella, with polite apologies, excused herself, and took her cousin away.

Had Basil not been quite so irritated at Isabella's casual leavetaking and a little stunned by her cousin's good looks, he might have noticed his friend's condition sooner. As it was, the viscountess made several attempts to return to discussion of the greys, and several times elicited only stuttering and confused replies from Freddie, before Basil noted anything amiss. He then calmly took over the conversation, brought it to a graceful close, and took his friend and himself away.

"It really is too bad of you, I must say," Basil remarked as they made their way to their club.

"Eh?" Lord Tuttlehope awoke from his stupor with a start.

"I said, it really is too bad of you."

"What is? Were you speaking, Trev?" Freddie shook his head. "Must have been woolgathering. Too bad—what?"

Basil clapped his friend on the shoulder and laughed. Freddie endured this for a moment, then responded, with some annoyance, "I say, Trev, fellow deserves to know what the joke is."

"Ah, my friend, I fear the joke is on me. I had new hopes. For a vision entered my life, complete with fortune, but younger, prettier, and, I think, far more susceptible than the icy Miss Latham. But what do you think? I look over and see that my bosom bow is struck on the spot, instantly besotted. Did you ever hear of worse luck?"

"Oh, Bella, what lovely gentlemen. I've never seen such cravats. Are they in love with you?"

"The gentlemen or the cravats?" Isabella asked, laughing.

Alicia's wardrobe for the Season covered every stick of

furniture in her room: walking dresses, pelisses, gowns, slippers, shawls. All had been inspected, tried on, exclaimed over, and the two women now sat on the bed, resting from their exertions.

"But are they? They're so handsome." Alicia sighed. "And so beautifully dressed."

"Yes, they're impeccable," replied her cousin. "And not, you goose, in love with me. Why, I'm quite an elderly lady. Your ancient companion, remember."

"Fah." The blonde curls shook a negative. "The only reason you're not married is that you've been buried in the country all this time taking care of us and helping Papa. I knew the minute you came to London you'd have dozens of *beaux*. Even Papa said so—when Mama was not about. Polly said at least a dozen came today. Even the Earl of Hartleigh." She pronounced this last with some awe.

Isabella's heart gave a little flutter, but she took a deep breath and told her cousin, "That is only etiquette, my dear."

This was not sufficient explanation, for her cousin must hear all the particulars of the Duchess of Chilworth's ball.

"And the dark-haired one, who looked so shy?" Alicia asked, shyly enough herself, when her cousin had finished detailing the previous evening.

"Where Mr Trevelyan goes, there goes Lord Tuttlehope. I assure you he hasn't the remotest interest in me."

"Oh." Alicia became thoughtful. If Lord Tuttlehope could have seen the tiny wrinkle between her brows or the charming way she chewed delicately on her lower lip, his fate would have been sealed.

But fortunately for that bewildered lord, there was only Isabella to see. She was curious about this interest in Basil's loyal companion, but had no opportunity to question her cousin, for Veronica entered then, demanding to see all the new finery. The wardrobe was displayed again, and Isabella soon left the two girls to their fantasies.

As the younger girls waited in happy anticipation of their

special day—practising the most killing ways of plying their fans, inventing witty retorts to imagined compliments, investigating the festive arrangements, and generally getting in the way of the servants, by whom they were frequently in danger of being trodden underfoot—Isabella continued to make the rounds with her aunt.

She went again to Almack's, where she found herself at the center of a small but enthusiastic circle of admirers. This was in marked contrast to her previous experience within those hallowed halls, when only the patronesses' benevolent tyranny had saved her from sitting out the entire evening. Then she had been matched up with bored but polite gentlemen who did their duty, suppressed their yawns, and then went on to more attractive game. Now, however, she was stalked not only by the persistent Basil, but also by a select group of other gentlemen with pockets to let.

In the course of her engagements, she had regularly found Lord Hartleigh gazing down at her in that tight, courteous, yet somehow disapproving way of his. He would never spend more than a few minutes with her—perhaps a single dance, or some polite social chatter. And then he would be gone. She noticed that he divided his attention among half a dozen young ladies, all of whom had similar credentials: good looks and breeding. Their bloodlines were no doubt as impeccable as those of his horses, and she wondered sardonically if he were evaluating them in the same way he would his cattle. So far, Lady Honoria Crofton-Ash seemed to have the advantage of her competitors, for he had danced twice with her this evening and brought her a lemonade. Isabella shrugged. The Marriage Mart was no different from Tattersall's. She only hoped that this cold and calculating business would not hurt Alicia. More than once she'd pictured her young cousin being snubbed by some overly fastidious member of the ton. More than once she had shook her head over her Aunt Pamela's obsession with status.

Well, it was too late now. Alicia would be thrust into Society, whether Society liked it or not, and she would have to endure the snubs and the slights. But Alicia was resilient. And intelligent. Perhaps less naïve than she seemed—for she had an uncanny knack of knowing when Lord Tuttlehope was visiting, and would manage to be seen. Perhaps she would simply pass by the door, conversing with her cousin or her abigail. Or perhaps she would stop in for a moment with an innocent question. These glimpses of the young lady seemed to leave Lord Tuttlehope in a state of stupefaction. He was inevitably tongue-tied if Alicia spoke one word to him.

Isabella smiled. There was evidence of mutual interest. If only Lord Tuttlehope's presence did not automatically signal that of his ever-present companion. Isabella awoke from her musings as Basil's shadow fell upon her. He had come to claim his dance. Ah, well. One must make the best of it, for Alicia's sake. If Basil persisted in trailing herself, then Lord Tuttlehope would not be far behind.

"Is it as dull as all that?" Basil asked as they took their places in the set.

"I beg your pardon?"

"Dull, Miss Latham. Though all at Almack's must *feel* it—at least those of any sensibility—you are the only woman here who clearly appears to wish she were elsewhere. In fact, so determined are you to be elsewhere that you travel there in spirit. It must be very dull indeed."

Firmly, Isabella brought her mind back from Alicia and *her* future to the present moment. "I assure you, sir, that this is all highly entertaining, and I was only tucking some observations into the back of my mind for later contemplation."

"Fortunate woman. I must do my contemplating now, and make the best of too few, too short hours," he murmured, as the requirements of the dance separated them.

She felt his eyes follow her as she moved away, and when, once or twice, she caught the intensity of his glance, she was forced to look away, suddenly feeling hot and angry. He had no business to stare after her in that way. It was most improper, and made her conspicuous.

When she rejoined him, she spoke out bluntly. "Mr Trevelyan, it is most inconsiderate of you to stare at me in that hungry fashion. Lady Jersey is watching you and is bound to make a story of it."

"*Hungry*, Miss Latham?" he queried, raising an eyebrow. "Your language is certainly most . . . most refreshing," he added with a chuckle.

"I have an unhappy habit of saying what I think—"

"And I an unhappy habit of showing what I feel." The topaz eyes narrowed, looking more catlike than ever. "But I beg your pardon. I did not wish to embarrass you."

Although she somehow suspected that he *did* wish to embarrass her—or at least to make her uncomfortable—she dared not contradict. She was afraid that he was only too eager to explain his motives. Abruptly, she changed the subject, asking after his aunt.

"Oh, Aunt Clem's quite well—in her element, in fact—busy at finding a suitable wife for my cousin." Another would not have noticed the way her smile froze on her face, but Basil was watching her closely. He noted her reactions as carefully as he would those of his opponents in a card game.

"Is it so massive an undertaking?" she asked, wondering why she suddenly felt unwell.

"She's been after him to marry since he returned to England. Responsibility, you know. Carry on the title and all that. But it's only since Lucy came into his care that he's shown any signs of enthusiasm." He glanced in the direction of a handsome young woman in ivory silk with whom Lord Hartleigh was conversing. "Though it may be too early to tell, I'd wager that Lady Honoria will be the lucky bride."

Reluctantly, Isabella followed the direction of his gaze. Yes, the earl *was* paying rather special attention to Lady Honoria. But then, what concern was it of hers?

Basil did not like what he was discovering, but persisted, nonetheless. For one, her discomfort compensated somewhat for his; and for another, well, he preferred to know exactly how the land lay. Thus she was relieved of hearing about Lord Hartleigh's matrimonial prospects and the wagers at White's on Lady Honoria's chances only when the dance separated them. When it finally ended, she urgently longed to be home again.

Unfortunately, the viscountess was enjoying a comfortable cose with Lady Cowper and clearly had no thoughts of departing. And then, as Basil brought Isabella back to her aunt, Lord Hartleigh appeared. This time Isabella was struck by the animosity between the two men. Oh, they were impeccably polite to each other, but the air fairly crackled with the tension between them. And when Lord Hartleigh led her away to dance, she knew that an angry pair of cat eyes followed them, watching every move.

Lord Hartleigh was not happy. He'd found himself walking toward her in spite of every intention of going in the opposite direction. For to speak with her meant enduring the presence of his insufferable cousin. Each and every time he'd seen her, he'd vowed to stay away. Yet each and every time, there she'd be, with Basil hovering nearby or stalking her with his eyes—and she looked so . . . so . . . in need of rescue, confound it! So the earl, relinquishing Lady Honoria to his rivals, would rescue Miss Latham, only to meet with, not gratitude, but an uneasy acquiescence. As though she mistrusted him as well. In fact, it was much the way in which Lucy looked at him. . . . Isabella's voice called him from his meditations. "I beg your pardon?" he responded.

"I was asking after your ward. I trust she's well?" Why did he ask her to dance if he was going to be so inattentive? Really, it was too bad. One cousin making her conspicuous by trailing her like a shadow and staring her out of countenance, and the other barely aware that she was alive—even when he danced with her.

"Quite well," he assured her. "At least in health," he added, after a moment. She was nonplussed to find him gazing down seriously at her, and wondered at the flicker of pain in his dark eyes. "I have little experience of children, yet it's clear to me she's unhappy." *Lonely*, he wanted to say. But to admit that the child was lonely, when everyone from the butler to the lowest scullery maid doted upon her, implied something wanting in himself.

"I think it's to be expected. The child still misses her parents, and her world now is vastly different from the world she knew. It will take time."

As she smiled up at him reassuringly, his throat tightened. "I hope that is all it is. . . ." His voice trailed off as he forced himself to look elsewhere—anywhere else—and thus met Lady Honoria's quizzical glance. He didn't mention that Lucy had asked for "Missbella" several times. Or that she had taken to none of the doting staff as she had taken to Miss Latham. Or that he had berated himself a thousand times for his behaviour that day at the dressmaker's—for had he been kinder and more patient, he might have learned Miss Latham's secret, and would not have this sad little ghost wandering aimlessly among her new toys and frocks. He mentioned none of these things, but they gnawed at him as he asked after Miss Latham's family and sought her impressions of London, now that she'd spent some weeks in town.

He was surprised to discover that her view of London had little to do with the balls and routs, the dinner parties and assemblies, the fashions and latest *on-dits* that occupied the minds of the women on his aunt's "list." Isabella Latham was a different species, who spoke intelligently of books and art and even—gracious heavens!—politics; who could not for the life of her remember Brummel's latest witticism or Caro Lamb's most recent misbehaviour.

As he led her back to her aunt (and the infernal Basil), he puzzled over this odd young lady. Clearly, she had no thought of herself as a belated debutante—in marked contrast to Miss Elderbridge, now in her seventh Season. To Isabella Latham, this London visit was a practical matter of overseeing her cousins' first Season: no more, no less. Apparently, her small crowd of admirers was, to her, a puzzling nuisance, and (except for Basil) about as troublesome to her equanimity as ants at a picnic. A curious, clearheaded, competent female, he thought . . . so why did she look so devilish unhappy and vulnerable as Basil bent to whisper in her ear?

4

"Well, my love, it seems you have decided to take the shine out of your cousins' debut by snatching up all their *beaux* beforehand."

Isabella looked up in surprise from the neat hem she was stitching. She had thought her mother was asleep on the sofa among her many pillows. "Mama, whatever are you talking about?"

Maria sighed. "It wants less than a week until our grand ball, and the house has been so overrun with your suitors that one hardly knows where to turn. I have not had a moment to myself to think."

What her mother possibly needed to think about, Isabella could not fathom. Lady Belcomb and Isabella had shared all the labour of preparing for the ball and making peace among the staff, while Mama's sole contribution had been an opinion of the colour of Alicia's gown.

"I do not recollect our being overrun by anything but servants, Mama. They are always so dreadfully in the way."

"Don't be coy with your mother, Isabella. Here is Mr Trevelyan stopping by nearly every single day with his friend—the one who prates so interminably of horses." Another sigh. "Your father never showed the least interest in horses, Isabella, I am relieved to inform you."

Nor had he ever evidenced much interest in anything else, thought Isabella. Not his business, nor his daughter; and barely his wife—though (she glanced at the still-beautiful woman reclining languidly among the pillows) Mama may not have been the most stimulating of companions.

"At any rate," her mother went on, "as if that were not fatiguing enough, they are soon followed by a host of dandies and other fine gentlemen. And then comes that tall young man—Lord Hartleigh, is it?"

Isabella nodded, and bent quickly again to her sewing.

"And he was here again today, asking after you. I'm afraid your Aunt Charlotte is quite vexed."

A quick scan of her parent's features showed no evidence of distress at this state of affairs.

"He stayed only a few minutes, you know. And Charlotte was very cross with me after. You must not run about London breaking hearts, my love. It is very tiresome for your cousins." A throaty chuckle accompanied this last. It was a sound very much like that which had not long ago so overset the Earl of Hartleigh—who might have been relieved to learn that it was merely a family trait (like hair colour), and not some cruel siren trick.

"I'm sorry, Mama. I shall try to restrain myself in the future."

"Do, love. You have no idea how your aunt frets about these poor gentlemen. And I do sympathise. One can become quite suffocated with all these *beaux* sighing about the house." In illustration, she sighed once again.

"Mama," said Isabella firmly, "for one, if anyone is to suffocate us, it is the servants. For another, you know as well as I do that nobody is sighing, and certainly not on my account. And for a third—"

"I pray you will not indulge in higher mathematics, Isabella—"

"For a third," her daughter went on, "this is a light spring shower compared to the deluge we may expect after Veronica and Alicia come out. And for a fourth—Mama, you are the most dreadful tease!"

"Yes, I know, darling. I can't help it." Mrs Latham pulled herself up to a sitting position and invited her daughter to join her on the sofa. As soon as they were settled, she said, patting Isabella's hand, "We must speak seriously, my dear.

About two matters. First, you were very naughty not to tell your aunt about your first meeting with Lord Hartleigh. She has got wind of it from the servants and told me that when he came today she did not know where to look, she was so moritifed." A low chuckle indicated the extent to which Maria sympathised with her sister-in-law.

"Oh dear, Mama. I'm sorry I didn't tell you, but I was sure there would be a fuss and I just wanted to forget the whole episode." Isabella flushed. "I do hope Aunt Charlotte said nothing to Lord Hartleigh about it. . . ."

"No, my love, she said all she had to say to me; at considerable length, I might add. But no matter. Apparently Lord Hartleigh bears no grudges." She gave her daughter a sidelong glance. "As I am sure you do not, Isabella—for it is quite wicked, you know, to bear a grudge."

"Yes, Mama."

"But to the other matter. What of his charming cousin? From what I have heard, he suffers from an excess of creditors. Not that there is anything so unusual in that." Maria paused, apparently distracted by another thought. "And if there is affection, of course—"

"I believe he is simply after my money," Isabella responded softly.

"In that case, perhaps you might send him about his business?"

"Perhaps."

"Unless you are fond of him," Maria added, as though she had not heard her daughter's reply.

"No."

"At any rate, you do not lack *other* suitors."

"Mama, they are *all* in love with my income," Isabella cried. "Every impoverished gentleman in London has put his name on my dance card and made his call. I have had so many offers to ride in the park that I cocculd spend the next ninety years in curricles, with my feet never once touching the earth." Though she spoke ironically, her eyes began to glisten with tears, which she determinedly withheld.

"How peculiar that so many impoverished young men should have so many curricles," her mother noted abstractedly.

"I am sure the money lenders do not find it peculiar at all."

"You are right, my dear. Money lenders understand everything, even the most inscrutable. But that was not my point; or was it? No. What I meant was that many of these young gentlemen are perfectly respectable—although, admittedly, unfortunate in having elder brothers. But Mr Trevelyan's reputation, from what I can gather—and that is mostly from the servants, for your aunt prefers to look smug—at any rate, his reputation is not entirely, shall I say, 'sunny'?"

Isabella gave a rueful little smile. "Perhaps that's why I find him the least abhorrent."

"My love, you are not turning romantic, are you? You have not been reading *Childe Harold* again? For you know your aunt will not have Byron's works in the house."

Isabella laughed in spite of herself. "No, Mama. It is just that if I must choose among fortune hunters, I would rather they be clever and charming—and wickedly attractive," she finished with a nervous giggle.

"I see."

Isabella had the feeling that her mother saw rather more than what had been spoken, but could not read in her face what it was.

"Well, then, go back to your stitching, though how your eyes can bear it I shall never know. I hope you will not wrinkle up on me, darling. Ah well, I suppose there's no stopping you. At any rate, I shall not tease you for at least the next hour. I am fearfully tired and must have a nap."

The wickedly attractive gentleman in question was in the process of being scolded—exactly like a naughty child—by his only partially indulgent aunt. He lounged carelessly against the ornate mantelpiece as, for the eighteenth time in one hour, she stressed the necessity of his getting his affairs in hand. In vain did he protest, his face absurdly innocent, that this was exactly what he'd been doing.

"Attempting to entrap a well-bred lady worth twenty of you in intelligence and good sense is not quite what I had in mind, you horrid boy." Lady Bertram was glaring at him most ferociously, but he did not cower; instead, he managed (though it hardly seemed possible) to look even more innocent. He was imagining himself a persecuted Muslim facing the Spanish Inquisition.

"Aunt Clem," he told her patiently, "I have been so prodigiously proper that it fair makes my hair stand on end. I have not spent a minute with the young woman when there were not at least half a dozen others standing watch in the same room—if not her aunt or her mother or her giggling cousin, then the servants. Belcomb has more footmen than he has furniture, you know. If anyone should feel entrapped, it should be myself."

This was met with a derisive snort.

"And I do not see, dearest Aunt, why you are so concerned with Miss Latham. Why, you are quite maternal—a veritable lioness defending her cub. Frightfully disloyal of you, you know. After all, *I* am your cub, or rather, one of them."

"Stuff! I like the gel, and won't see her made miserable for life. Bad enough her mother made such a mull of things."

While Basil did not find this response especially flattering, he was too aware of his own failings to contradict. More than likely he *would* make a wife miserable, and her misery would increase in proportion to her intelligence. That promised Miss Latham a thoroughly wretched future. Unfortunately, Basil hadn't enough conscience to overcome his self-interest. While he knew of several wealthy—and vulgar—peageese who might look upon him with favour, he had already spent much precious time cultivating Miss

Latham and couldn't afford to start afresh with someone else. He would have preferred, certainly, to see a bit more evidence that she was succumbing to his charm. The creditors were beginning to raise a nasty clamour; and the way she watched Edward when she thought no one was looking was not at all encouraging to their interests. Even less encouraging was that Edward watched her in the same manner. This made Basil anxious, a state of mind entirely foreign to his nature and, oddly enough, not the least bit refreshing.

He ran his fingers through his tawny hair, making its carefully arranged windblown appearance more genuinely tousled. He did wish Aunt Clem would leave off scolding. For here was a tailor's bill in his pocket which, if not paid up by tomorrow, would render his current wardrobe his final one. And in frayed collars, limp neckcloths, and threadbare waistcoats, one could not expect to charm wealthy young ladies or allay the fears of their relatives. He offered his aunt a lazy smile. "Ah, her mother. But you know, Aunt, I suspect she hadn't the energy to make a mull of things. They must have simply mulled themselves."

"You know nothing of it. She was quite a lively girl in her youth. But her life in later years wore her down. As it will, you know." Lady Bertram spared her nephew a meaningful look before returning to her reminiscences. "What a pity she and Harry Deverell couldn't have made a match of it. You know," she mused, partly to herself, "I never did understand what made her run off with Latham."

Basil was all curiosity, the tailor momentarily forgotten. "You mean there was something between Mrs Latham and the new viscount? The one everyone thought dead all these years?"

The sharp brown eyes considered him, and a sad, patient look passed briefly across the aristocratic features. "No, that's not what I meant at all. They grew up together and were like brother and sister. And even if their feelings had been more romantic, it would have been impractical, of course. Neither family was well off."

"You see, Aunt? Even you realise that one can't live on affection alone. The grocer must be paid. . . ."

"And the tailor, too, I suppose. Don't play the innocent with me, you villainous boy," she went on, in response to his upraised eyebrow. "My sources tell me that Mr Stutts refuses to extend you any further credit."

"Aunt Clem sees all, knows all," replied the villainous boy, with some relief.

"Of course I do, you young jackanapes. Well, then, what will it take to pacify him?"

Now *this* was interesting, Basil thought, as he strolled down Saint James's. Harry Deverell and the languid Mrs Latham had grown up together. And yet, when the story about the mysterious viscount had come up in conversation, she had barely attended. But then, whenever she did put in one of her rare appearances, she seldom seemed to attend to anything. And every time Basil saw her, he was hard put to connect her darker, striking beauty with her daughter's pale, nearly nondescript features. Must take after the father, he thought. And yet that side of the family, too—if Alicia was the rule, rather than the exception—certainly was more strikingly handsome. Well, one could not always rely on family resemblances. Although that had sealed the mysterious viscount's fate, hadn't it? Basil cast his mind back, trying to recall the story that had had London in such an uproar . . . when was it, a year ago?

Harry Deverell, youngest son of Andrew, Viscount Deverell, had gone to sea. Evidently, he was not the clerical type of younger son, for he had decided on a distinctly hazardous mode of getting his living. But his career was cut short when he fell overboard in a sudden storm off the Cornish coast, and he was presumed drowned.

It turned out, however, that he'd been able, by some miracle, to make his way to shore, where he was rescued by some folk or other—smugglers, no doubt, as they all were thereabouts. Severely weakened by his efforts, he'd fallen seriously ill, and when the fever and delirium finally left him, several weeks later, he could remember nothing, not even his name. Only his sailor's garb offered any clue, and he returned to his trade, hoping this would help him recall his lost past.

From then on, he'd travelled the globe as an obscure sailor, never crossing paths with any who might recognise him. It was only when he finally settled in India—some five years ago—that he had contact with any of his class. But by then, Harry Deverell had been so long thought dead that even those noting a family resemblance would not connect him with the retired Captain Williams.

And then it happened that one who had seen him commented on this resemblance to an acquaintance about to assume a post in the same Indian town. Upon arriving, Sir Philip Pomfret had promptly looked up Captain Williams, remarked the resemblance himself, and instituted an inquiry into the captain's history. The timing of the accident at sea, coupled with the physical evidence . . . All the evidence pointed to one conclusion. But when confronted with this information, Captain Williams joked it all away, saying that dozens of men had been lost off the Cornish coast in one endeavour or another, and he was as likely the son of a low smuggler as of the late viscount.

Yet there was nothing low or common about Captain Williams. And when word eventually reached Sir Philip that the two eldest Deverell sons had been killed in a carriage accident, he took the captain aside and made a passionate appeal to his sense of duty: "If you are *not* Harry Deverell, then you have nothing to gain or lose. But if you are, it is your duty to see to the welfare of your brothers' widows and daughters, who have next to nothing to live on."

Thus Captain Williams was persuaded to write to the family solicitor. That dedicated old gentleman, struck by the familiar handwriting, promptly embarked on a long and grueling voyage to India. He recognised Harry immediately. And his persuasions, coupled with those of Sir Philip, at length convinced the captain to assume his rightful identity and the title. Commitments in India made it impossible for the new viscount to return home with the solicitor, but he was to follow in some months. And the Deverells—what was left of them—were expecting him back anytime now.

Handsome, dashing—so Aunt Clem had described Harry Deverell, dwelling at such length on his fair hair and captivating blue eyes, which darkened or lightened with his mood (not to mention his tall, slim, muscular physique), that Basil had to tease her about nursing a secret *tendre* for young Harry. But Aunt Clem had only smiled wickedly, and reminded her nephew that she'd had her own handsome devil to reform.

Yet this attractive fellow had never married. Too wily to be caught in the parson's mousetrap?

"Maybe too honourable," Aunt Clem had replied. "For how could he know he was not already wed?"

"In that case, he does not seem to have exerted himself to discover his supposed widow—or anything at all about his lost past."

Aunt Clem had shrugged, saying that one did not know all the circumstances.

No, thought Basil, one did not. But it would be amusing to find out about Mrs Latham's former playfellow. At the very least, it would be a diversion from this, so far, unsuccessful assault on Isabella Latham's heart. And after all, there may be other ways to win her golden guineas than by winning her heart.

5

About the time a certain Bond Street tailor's troubled spirit was being soothed by an injection of guineas, Lord Hartleigh (his own tailor in a permanently ecstatic state) was strolling in the park with a most fetching unmarried young lady. No groom or maid trailed behind the attractive couple, and one or two persons, who had ventured into the park at this early hour for interesting purposes of their own, stopped to stare.

Lord Hartleigh was feeling rather foolish, for his companion did not seem to find him stimulating. Nor did her new cherry frock, brilliant with ribbons and lace, cheer her. Her dark curls tumbled about a most lachrymose visage, and she plodded sadly and silently along beside him, looking up obediently from time to time as he pointed out various sights.

"Are you tired, Lucy?" the earl at length inquired.

"No, Uncle Edward," she murmured.

"Perhaps you'd prefer to visit another place?"

"No, thank you, Uncle Edward."

Blast! There was no pleasing the child. In response to Aunt Clem's scathing remarks regarding "that suffocating house," he had begun trotting his ward from one London sight to another. But nothing had lifted her spirits—not the balloon ascension, not Astley's Circus, not even the British Museum with its odd assortment of curiosities. In every case, she accompanied her handsome guardian in the same obedient but sad, limp manner.

"Perhaps you'd like to play with the other children," he suggested in desperation, gesturing toward a distant section of the park where several nurses stood guard over their small charges.

Lucy dutifully looked in the direction he indicated, and was about to utter another polite refusal when she spied a young woman sitting, sketching, beneath a tree. "It's Miss-bella!" she exclaimed, looking up eagerly at her guardian. She began tugging at his hand. "May we see her, please, Uncle Edward? It's *Missbella!*" With unexpected strength, the tiny hands were pulling him in the direction of the tree, and he found himself obediently following.

When they were yet several yards away, Lucy broke free of her guardian's grip and raced toward the young woman. She flung herself upon the startled Isabella, nearly knocking the wind out of her with the eagerness of her hugs as she cried, "I found you! I found you!"

"Why, Lucy," the lady gasped, "what a lovely surprise."

"Lucy, I'm afraid you are crushing Miss Latham."

Isabella looked up from the mass of tumbled curls and cherry ribbons to see the earl frowning down at her. Her pulse quickened, and she blushed. "Lord Hartleigh. Good morning."

In prompt response to her flushed cheeks came the odd sensation in his chest again. As if this affliction were not bad enough, it was now aggravated by the fierce tweak of Envy. Lucy's face glowed as she held on tenaciously to her friend. She loosed her embrace only enough to begin an animated cross-examination. She asked a hundred questions and answered them all herself. She demanded to know where Isabella had been and why she had not come to see her. And she repeated for Isabella's enlightenment all that the earl had taught her about the park and its environs. The child's sudden loquaciousness and uninhibited display of affection toward Miss Latham was most surprising—and not altogether flattering to Lord Hartleigh.

Isabella seemed to sense this. After responding as well

as she could to this barrage, she suggested that Lucy release her so that she might converse with her guardian, who was, she noted, being rather impolitely ignored. Thus gently chastised, Lucy let go. As Isabella began to struggle to her feet, Lord Hartleigh waved her back.

"Pray do not rise on our account, Miss Latham. I see you had been working most comfortably until our somewhat precipitate arrival." That said, he gracefully dropped down to sit beside them, careless of the grass stains and dirt that would later torment his valet.

"I'm afraid it is not work, precisely," Isabella explained, greatly flustered by the proximity of his long, lean body. "Usually I ride in the morning. But my groom could not be spared today. So here I am, making ladylike little sketches. It offers a change." In response to his quizzical look, she went on, nervously, "We are in a turmoil with preparations for my cousins' debut, you see, and I occasionally must come away, to escape the servants and restore my sense of perspective."

"And no doubt to escape the press of morning callers," he added ironically, and then promptly regretted it. He *wished* she would not blush so easily. It had a mischievous effect on his breathing apparatus, which seemed to have suddenly shut down.

"I—I believe I mentioned that I am unused to fine company," she stammered. There was that stern gaze again. Why must he look so very disapproving?

"I beg your pardon, Miss Latham. I did not mean to imply. . . ." But he didn't know what he didn't mean, and found himself at a loss to continue.

Fortunately, Lucy was subject to no such hesitation. She was oblivious to the grown-ups' discomfort and had grown impatient for the lady's attention. "I missed you so much," she announced, once more flinging her arms around Isabella's neck. "Uncle Edward takes me to see so many things." She went on, to her guardian's amazement, to list every sight and repeat, virtually word for word, all that he

46

had told her. He never believed she'd been attending to his commentaries at all. Yet his face did not betray his surprise; it seemed only to grow more stern.

"And now you must come, too," the child insisted. "You will come, won't you?"

Since the earl did not appear nearly so eager as his ward, Isabella was puzzled how to respond. "Well, you see, Lucy," she began, hesitantly, "we are very busy at home just now, and I am not quite sure when it would be possible. Perhaps in a few weeks. . . ." Her voice trailed off, her cheeks pink again. At this, the child's eyes began to glisten dangerously, and Isabella hugged her closer. "And besides," she added softly, "you did not think perhaps that your guardian would like to have you all to himself?"

The hazel eyes looked out from beneath the curls to that gentleman's stern visage, and then turned back to gaze at Isabella in incredulity. Her expression did not escape her guardian, who managed to force out, past whatever inside was trying to strangle him, that he would be honoured if Miss Latham would consent to accompany them one day; and that if there were time in her busy schedule, perhaps she would join them in their visit to an exhibition of landscapes. "I thought the scenes would be more interesting to Lucy than fashionable portraits," he explained. "I—I know she misses the country." His expression softened as he regarded his ward, and Isabella glimpsed something in his eyes that made her feel a twinge of sympathy.

"I should be delighted."

"Is tomorrow too soon?" Lord Hartleigh ventured.

Tomorrow was not too soon. A time being settled upon, and arrangements made for the earl's carriage to stop for her, Lord Hartleigh endeavoured to dislodge his young companion. "Lucy, I am certain Miss Latham cannot breathe when you clutch at her in that way." He did not add that, Lucy having disarranged Miss Latham's hair, various blond tendrils had escaped to tickle a delicate pink ear in the most enticing fashion. . . . He collected himself with a start. "We must leave her in peace now—else she may not wish to see us again tomorrow."

Miss Latham was not destined to be left in peace, however, for her Nemesis (so Basil had come to style himself) was not far behind his cousin. He had come to the park in response to an urgent message from an elegant young woman with creditors of her own to soothe. When Mr Trevelyan informed the lovely Celestine—with beautifully phrased regret—that the creditors simply had to wait, this interesting meeting had come to an abrupt end. He therefore decided to devote the remainder of a fine morning to planning the next stage of his assault on the Answer to His Prayers. A broken heart, he decided, was best. He would simply commence to pine away, and let guilt lead her to the altar. He had been staring at the pond, wondering whether an attempted suicide by drowning would be overly theatrical, when his eye caught a flash of colour from the trees beyond. He made out—at some distance—his cousin, engaged in a *tête-à-tête* with Miss Latham. Now here was an unseemly state of affairs: his Intended conversing with a fashionable gentleman and no abigail in sight. Unless you counted as a chaperone the moppet bouncing up and down on her bosom. Thinking of that bosom, he gave a little sigh. Then, realising there was no one about to hear it, he left off sighing and backed away into a more sheltered spot from which he might await his own turn.

He hadn't long to wait. Edward rose; the moppet ceased bouncing and was led away. Livelier than she was last time I saw her, Basil thought as he watched her skip along next to her guardian.

As soon as they were out of sight, he sauntered casually around the pond and, in no apparent hurry, made his way to Isabella's side. A glance back told him that they were not in view of the diverse nurses and their charges.

Not having noticed his approach—no doubt preoccupied with the recent conversation and, in particular, the earl's warm brown eyes—Isabella looked up, bewildered, at his greeting.

"I see you, too, have decided to take advantage of this brilliant morning," Basil observed, peering down over her shoulder at the neglected sketch pad. "But you will make a long job of it without your pencil." And without waiting for an invitation, he flung himself down on the ground beside her.

She had not yet had the experience of being alone with Mr Trevelyan and, considering his disconcerting effect on her when others were about, did not intend to broaden her education. "I was just preparing to leave. . . ," she began, turning away from the cat eyes to search for her pencil, which had rolled away into the grass.

"And leave me to my lonely meditations? Yet I fear it is no more than I deserve."

"It is not on your account, Mr Trevelyan," she snapped. It was exceedingly uncomfortable to find him so close. "I have stayed overlong as it is, only I do not know where Polly can have got to. She has been gone this half hour at least."

After amiably suggesting that Polly must have drowned herself, Basil added blandly, "But see, you have had Lord Hartleigh as sentinel, and now that he is gone, here am I to take my turn as your protector."

For what seemed the thousandth time that morning, Isabella felt her face grow hot, but she forced herself to meet his gaze. It was an unsettling experience. The topaz eyes studied her, waiting. He reminded her of a cat crouched, ready to spring. Only he wasn't crouching. He was sitting, leaning back against the tree. "Lord Hartleigh was only trying to please his ward. She has taken a sudden . . . liking to me," she said, faltering.

"That is not in the least surprising. But my cousin should beware. The condition is contagious." Considerate of the moppet to have a wrestle with Miss Latham, for that lady's coiffure was in a most appealing state of disarray. A stray cherry-coloured ribbon dangling from her sleeve caught his eye. Apparently without thinking, he lifted it away, but she started at his touch. "Why, Miss Latham," he drawled, "I believe the child has frazzled your nerves. I'm sure I told you I won't bite. I was merely relieving you of this . . . love token she left behind."

"I shall return it to her," said Isabella, reaching to take it. But he snatched his hand away and pocketed the ribbon.

"Although I am all curiosity as to *when* you would have the opportunity, I shall keep in mind what happens to curious cats, and content myself with retaining this—as *my* love token."

"Mr Trevelyan, you have a highly overactive imagination." Hurriedly, she began gathering up her belongings, preparing to rise. His hand on her arm stopped her. "I wish you would not leave," he said softly.

Her heart began to pound. The voice and eyes were hypnotic, tempting her in spite of herself. She had only to pull herself free of his grasp. Yet she couldn't, or wouldn't. She had only to say a word to send him about his business, as Mama had suggested, but the word would not come. She had the curious sensation of observing herself, as though in a dream, as the sleepy cat eyes grew larger and seemed to swallow her up, as his fingers touched her cheek, and as she felt his lips on her own. For a moment all thought left her and time hung suspended. The sketchbook dropped from her hands. She felt his arms around her, pulling her closer, his mouth insistent. She felt his heart thudding next to her own. And then, as though from a tremendous distance, she heard a child's cry, and abruptly, the spell was broken. With all her strength, she thrust him away from her and struggled to her feet. He scrambled up after her, catching her before she could run away.

"Let go of me," she gasped.

"I will," he answered, a little breathless himself, "but you must not hate me. Isabella—"

"How dare you?" Angry tears welled up, and she had to bite her lip to keep from sobbing.

"I'm sorry I upset you. You must forgive me, Isabella. Here." He offered his handkerchief, which she angrily thrust away.

"Your m-manners leave a great deal to be desired."

"But my darling Isabella, I warned you I was not to be trusted. I told you I was perfectly dreadful. Even my aunt told you. Therefore, it is entirely your fault—"

"My fault?" He made her head spin. "You must be mad, and I madder still to stand here listening to your nonsense. And I am certainly not your darling," she snapped. "You may address me as 'Miss Latham'—if there is any occasion in future when I should be so idiotic as to permit you to address me at all."

"What you permit me to say aloud has no bearing on what I say in my heart. You *are* my darling. And my darling Isabella, you must compose yourself, for here comes your unreliable Polly, who has not drowned in the pond after all, and you don't wish to scandalise her."

Suspecting that the embrace had left physical evidence, she hastily endeavoured to restore herself to rights, and hoped that Lucy's enthusiasm would satisfy the abigail's curiosity as explanation for Isabella's dishevelled appearance. As she gathered her belongings and began to move away, he stopped her once more.

"You must say you forgive me, Isabella—"

"You are mad—"

"—for if you do not, I shall kiss you again, in full view of Polly."

Worried that Polly may already have had the pair in her sights, Isabella nodded, and struggled to break free of his grasp. He smiled as he released her, and watched as she hurried away.

The perfidious Polly was subjected to a scolding which left her as red-eyed as her mistress by the time they reached home. Declaring that she would see to her own hooks and buttons, and had too frightful a headache to eat nuncheon,

Isabella slammed the bedroom door on her maid, flung herself on the bed, and burst into tears.

What a horrid, horrid man! To leap upon her the moment they were alone—as though she were one of his ladybirds. Oh, she knew he had them. He had probably come direct from a tryst with one of them. And what had she been thinking of, to allow him to kiss her? Of course she knew it would be no polite peck on the cheek. What a perfect idiot she was! What if they had been seen?

Her face feeling as though it were in flames, she got up from the bed and went to the washstand to bathe her eyes and burning cheeks. The cool water helped calm her. As she forced herself to look into the mirror, she knew why she had not prevented his embrace. Madame Vernisse may have been a worker of miracles, but even her powers could not render Isabella Latham beautiful. Or even unusually pretty. There was nothing uncommon about her blue eyes. They were not violet, like those of the infamous Lady Delmont. And while the right light—or the right frock—might enhance their colour, they had no real depth, no real mystery. And it was highly improbable that they were "that deep blue of the Ionian sea, wherein a man might choose to drown himself," as Basil had recently assured her. If only he *would* drown himself, she thought crossly. But in doing so, he would drown the only romance that had ever or would ever enter her life. She stared critically at her reflexion as she angrily yanked the comb through her hair.

She was twenty-six years old. And until this poetically inclined fortune hunter had come along, no man had ever looked twice at her. Not, of course, that she'd had much contact with young men; first poverty, and then the work she was so happy to do for Uncle Henry, had kept her from socialising. Still, her own father had barely noticed when she was in the same room. And now, though a small army of men had besieged her, not one except Basil had so much as hinted, in look or word, that she (as opposed to her income) was desirable. Oh, they had flattered her, but not with hidden suggestion, as Basil had. And as to the flattery, one could not even enjoy it for what it was, knowing that their eyes lingered more lovingly—good heavens!—upon her *mother.*

Thus, though she knew it was foolish, Isabella had wanted not simply to be kissed, but for someone to *want* to kiss her. She had wanted to know what it was like. Only now she could hardly recollect what it was like, so overset was she with anger and shame. She took a deep breath and forced herself to remember. His hand had touched her cheek, bringing her face closer to his . . . and then his lips, soft on her own. And then? What had she felt? She closed her eyes, trying to recapture that moment. But all she could remember was his overwhelming physical presence and her own warring sensations of fear . . . and curiosity. It was not quite what she'd expected from an embrace. She hadn't even felt that rush of warmth she'd experienced when Lucy hugged her. And not . . . that tingle of excitement when Lord Hartleigh sat down beside her.

For that was what she'd been contemplating when Basil had come upon her. Lord Hartleigh. Oh, worse and worse. Lord Hartleigh, who only tolerated her to indulge his ward. Had Isabella actually believed one cousin might substitute for the other? The idea drove her tears away. "Isabella," she scolded her reflexion, "you are perfectly absurd."

And with that heartening thought to cheer her, she dried her tears, changed her clothes, and went down to join her family.

6

"Lord Hartleigh!" her aunt cried. "Taking you for a ride in his carriage? But that—"

"Is yet another one," Mama interjected, in an undertone.

It was at tea that Isabella had quietly announced her plans for the following day. Alicia had nearly knocked over the teapot in her excitement and had been about to bubble forth predictions concerning the earl's intentions when the viscountess's outraged response immediately subdued her.

"What is it that you are saying, Maria? You know one cannot understand you when you mumble."

"It was nothing, my dear sister. Arithmetic. Counting to myself."

"I cannot think why you should do figures when we are discussing this highly improper state of affairs."

The only indication of alarm Maria Latham gave at this pronouncement was a slight lifting of one eyebrow in disbelief. "I do not see what is so improper about Isabella being invited for a drive. You were not shocked when Mr Porter invited her—and I am sure that high-perched contrivance of his cannot be safe."

Isabella attempted to step into the crossfire. "We are not taking a drive through the park, Aunt Charlotte," she began to explain.

"What, have you rejected him too, my love?"

Now this was very naughty of Mama indeed. Lady Belcomb had not at all objected to the penurious suitors who crowded her drawing room every day the family was "at home." It was a convenient means of separating the wheat from the chaff, since, with neither looks nor charm, the only attraction Isabella could boast was her fortune. Those who called were therefore not at all the sort whose attentions one would wish upon Veronica. But Lord Hartleigh was not of this ilk. What doubly provoked the viscountess was that the earl seemed somehow beholden to Isabella on account of that absurd business with the little orphan.

And now here was Maria implying—with that studied innocence of hers—that the Earl of Hartleigh had been reduced to a state which rendered him vulnerable to *rejection,* and by a tradesman's daughter! The idea filled the viscountess with rage and, consequently, turned her face purple. She relieved her feelings by venting some of her wrath on her daughter.

"Veronica, I do wish you'd stop that dreadful noise," Lady Belcomb commanded, scowling at her. Under her parent's glare, Veronica quickly stifled her giggles and bowed her head to stare into her cup. Alicia, subduing her own mirth, bent her head likewise and endeavoured to look serious.

"Please, Aunt," Isabella interjected. "It is all very easily explained—and not a bit what you think." This being met by no other rejoinder than a "harrumph," she went on, "I believe you are aware that Lord Hartleigh has been named as guardian to the daughter of his very dear friend, who passed away a short time ago—"

"Such a sad business," Mama sighed.

"This ward," Isabella went on, with a brief frown at her irrepressible parent, "has taken a fancy to me; I am sure I don't know why. . . ."

"But, my love, you were always so good with children—even the most tiresome—"

"Mama, it is very difficult to hold my train of thought when you keep interrupting."

"Yes, Maria, do let her get on with it."

Murmuring an apology, Maria looked off toward the clock with an abstracted air.

"At any rate, the child has taken a fancy to me, and Lord Hartleigh—who, you can well imagine, is much at a loss to amuse a seven-year-old girl—"

A quelling glance from the viscountess squelched another of her daughter's giggling fits.

"—has invited me to this exhibition of landscapes *solely* to please the child, who insisted I bear them company."

There were some signs that Lady Belcomb was beginning to be appeased: Her face, for instance, was beginning to recover its normal colour. She was not entirely satisfied, however. "It seems to me, Isabella," she asserted, "that Lord Hartleigh is overly indulgent of his ward's whims."

"I am sure, Aunt, that is because he has had no experience of children. As he becomes more accustomed to his role, I am quite convinced he will be less indulgent."

"I would expect so. Nonetheless, I do not think he would take it much amiss if you were to indicate—tactfully, of course—that it is not at all to his ward's benefit to spoil her."

"At the very first opportunity," Isabella solemnly assured her aunt, while feeling quite convinced that the earl would take it very much amiss indeed.

"Well, then, I suppose we must at least commend Lord Hartleigh for wishing to do his duty by this orphan; although I do feel he has been carried away by his enthusiasm. But no matter. And you will take your abigail with you, Isabella?"

"I do not see why Polly must go as well. . . ," Maria began, but the viscountess's face began to darken again, and she lazily added, "but then I suppose a seven-year-old child cannot count as chaperone."

"Of course not, Mama."

"Then I suppose we must let her go, Maria," Lady Belcomb announced magnanimously.

"Oh, I suppose we must," her sister-in-law agreed with a sigh. "I only hope the child does not tire her overmuch."

And with the crisis resolved, the ladies returned to their

tea and managed to make a tolerable meal, despite the disagreeable necessity of having to shoo away diverse servants who persisted in duplicating one another's efforts, bustling in and out for no apparent reason, adding to and subtracting from the meal at their own whims.

It was not long after tea that Maria Latham entered her daughter's room. She was not wont to visit much, preferring to spend most of her time in her sitting room, where she could recline comfortably. Thus she was struck anew by the room's small size and inelegant decor. Gracefully, she dropped into a chair close by the little desk where Isabella sat composing a letter to her Uncle Henry. As she glanced about her at the threadbare furnishings, Maria lamented, "I do wish your aunt had selected another room for you, my love. These yellow draperies do not suit your complexion."

Isabella swallowed a smile. "I don't know where else she might put me, Mama. Veronica cannot be expected to share her room with Alicia, and certainly one could not squeeze so much as a mouse into the servants' quarters."

"Yes, I'm certain you are right, darling—although I'm afraid I must quarrel with any attempt to put you among the servants. But it is so distressing. I do not know whether it is the colour of the draperies that makes you appear so fatigued. Although, come to think of it, you appeared fatigued at tea as well. But of course, there was Charlotte being so very tiresome. Not to mention this distressing surfeit of servants. They quite exhaust me. It is no wonder Thomas could not afford a proper Season for your cousin, when he requires an army to run even such a modest place as this. At any rate, you must promise me that you will not allow this little girl to treat you as her hobby-horse. Polly tells me that the child made you most untidy. 'Like a big wind had blowed her from one end of London to the other' were her exact words, I believe."

Isabella could not meet her mother's eyes. "I'm sure Polly

was exaggerating, Mama," she managed to reply after what seemed like a monstrous long silence. "Lucy is very affectionate, and I believe she is very lonely—"

"No doubt," her mother replied, apparently engrossed in contemplation of a particularly inept sketch that hung by the door. As she brought her gaze back to her daughter, she went on, softly, "Still, it would not do for your aunt to see you return home tomorrow in the frazzled state Polly so vividly described."

"You are quite right, Mama. But as we are merely going to look at some pictures, Lucy will not have the opportunity to 'frazzle' me."

"Yes, that is so. Well, I believe I shall go to my own room and take a nap. Your aunt's lectures weary one so, and I do not see why she must be so disagreeable at tea. It is not at all recommended for the digestion." She patted her daughter's hand and rose to leave. But a few steps from the door, she stopped and said, as an afterthought, "By the way, Isabella, I do not recollect your mentioning meeting up with Mr Trevelyan as well as his cousin. But then, perhaps I was not listening as closely as I ought." She frowned once again at the offending sketch. "No matter. I should develop a headache as well as indigestion attempting to keep count of your *beaux*." And on that enigmatic note, she exited, leaving Isabella staring open-mouthed after her.

Miss Latham's was not the only equanimity to be ruffled by the morning's Adventure. Upon returning to his lodgings, Mr Trevelyan found himself uncharacteristically out of sorts. It was not the pricks of conscience which disturbed him, however; nor was it the tone of impatience which had crept into his landlady's heretofore respectful inquiry regarding several months' back rent. After all, Freddie could most likely be counted on to advance a small loan. But one could not much longer continue to exist on the good offices of friends and Aunt Clem, and the once extremely remote prospect of debtors' prison now loomed closer by the day. The prison walls cast a long cold shadow which seemed to draw the warmth from Basil's cramped rooms. What else had led him, on this beautiful spring afternoon, to build a fire near which he huddled, nursing a brandy?

His friends' experience had shown him that debtors' prison could be a tolerable place. There at least one was free of the harassments of creditors. Yet though it might be tolerable, he had no wish to avail himself of that species of liberty, and was just now wondering how his normally reliable instincts for survival had led him so far astray.

Patiently, he'd been insinuating himself, little by little, into Miss Latham's good graces. And the hints he'd dropped among his acquaintance had led many to believe that her virtue was teetering on the brink. But this morning he had risked it all—for what? A kiss. And now she would not only cease trusting him, but would more than likely refuse to have anything further to do with him. This could not improve his position with his creditors, who, like his gambling friends, had begun to believe he was on his way to a prosperous match.

As he absently turned the brandy glass in his hands, he realised that he might have mistaken his victim. Her plainness, her naïveté, and her idiotic relations had all led him to believe she was less well protected and would be more easily manipulated than other eligible young ladies. But she would only be led so far; she was still wary of him, still taken with Edward.

He gazed for a long time into the fire, watching the logs crackle and break, to send off bright, hot little sparks before they crumbled into ashes. Though Isabella was not an antidote, she certainly was not beautiful. Next to the sparkling good looks of her young cousins, she was a mouse. But there was something about her innocent, blunt way of reacting to him which was rather appealing.

There was an odd mixture of longing and defiance in the looks which accompanied her earnest scoldings, and these looks somehow tempted him. Today he had succumbed to temptation. The brief embrace showed that she was truly inexperienced, despite that insinuating laugh of hers. But tutoring her might be rather pleasant, for she was—though in the oddest way—*attractive.* He did not love her, but maybe in time might feel affection for her. And perhaps those attractions might even command his attention—at least now and then—over the interminable dreariness of marriage.

Yet one could hardly contemplate marriage when one's Intended refused to have anything further to do with one. What a fool he'd been. What would it be now? Go to Lord Belcomb, confess to compromising her, offer to repair the damage by marrying her? He paused, the glass halfway to his lips. Could he carry it off?

Not likely. True, her noble relations might agree to any nonsense he suggested. When Maria had run off with her cit, they'd coldly washed their hands of her. They'd do anything to prevent another scandal. After all, a second generation run amok would indicate something depraved in the blood. But Isabella was just as likely to pack up and return to her commercial uncle and bury herself in the country. Marry a scoundrel? On account of one stolen kiss in broad daylight? No. Something else must persuade her, and soon.

According to Freddie, Lord Hartleigh had called more than once for Isabella; and he *was* seeking a mama for Lucy. So either he was interested in Isabella on her own account or he was courting her on account of the moppet. Not that it made sense, for Edward could marry where he chose. And of course, if he chose Isabella, she'd have him. Then Basil would have to start afresh with another Answer to His Prayers, and that would take time. But time was running out.

In this unusual state of self-doubt, Basil continued until the fire had long died down and Freddie appeared, seeking company for dinner. As he waited for his friend to dress,

Lord Tuttlehope helped himself to a glass of brandy and settled himself in the chair Basil had vacated. When Basil reemerged, Freddie eyed him up and down. "See Stutts came up to snuff after all," he commented.

"The aunt, Freddie, whose generosity surpasseth understanding," Basil explained. "She has paid the tailor, in hopes that—in appearance, at least—her nephew will not disgrace her."

This led to a discussion of the cut of waistcoats and a review of their acquaintances' merits in this area.

"All in all," Freddie noted, "only one in the same race with you is Hartleigh. But all his valet's got to do is dress him." And thus casually discounting Lord Hartleigh's sartorial achievements, he went on. "By the way, heard he's taking Miss Latham to look at some pictures tomorrow. Never fancied art myself. Hunting scene's not a bit like the real thing, you know."

Basil, who had been regarding his reflexion in the glass with a certain degree of complacency, whirled around. At Lord Tuttlehope's blink, he turned back again, adjusted his neckcloth, and responded blandly, "Indeed? So you've been to see the Belcombs *et al.* on your own today."

"Well, yes. That is. . . . Well, you were engaged." Discomfited, Freddie blinked at his brandy glass several times.

"And were you rewarded, my friend? Did you catch a glimpse of the fair goddess?"

"What? Oh. Well, that is. . . ."

Basil was amused to see his companion's face turn red as a beet-root. He turned from the mirror and gave Freddie's shoulder a comforting pat. "Try to restrain your lyric tongue, my lad. At least to me. It will be better spent on the young lady." He poured himself another glass of brandy. "But I gather you heard something useful?"

"Didn't stay long. Ladyship was in a pet. Just saw Belcomb on the way to his club. Said she'd rung a peal over him. Asked me why his niece couldn't see Hartleigh if she liked. Free country."

And in this clipped fashion, with the help of patient questioning, Freddie told his friend what he wished to know.

"Deverell?" Lord Belcomb repeated, trying to put the name to a face he hadn't seen in over a quarter of a century. Absentminded, like his sister, Basil thought; yet quite different. Where Mrs Latham was languid, he was bluff and hearty. And where he was the bumbling sort who knew a great deal less than he thought he did, Mrs Latham seemed to understand rather more than she let on. Basil had more than once felt her considering gaze upon him, and looked up only to find her staring off at nothing in particular. Yes, of course all considered her perfectly harmless—perfectly useless, in fact—but somehow Basil's instincts warned him otherwise. And even now, as he pumped the viscount for information, he had the dim sensation of having strayed too far.

"Ah yes," Lord Belcomb recalled. "Young Harry. The fair-haired one. Fine lad. Pity he died so young. Or rather, not dead after all, eh?" He signalled for more brandy. Charlotte had been in one of her takings this evening, and he—as was his custom on such occasions—had beat a hasty retreat to his club. He'd not been exactly delighted to see Mr Trevelyan, for that young man was one of the subjects on which Charlotte dwelt at unmerciful length; as though it were the viscount's business to bring the man up to scratch. And why? Lord Belcomb wondered. For here was the Earl of Hartleigh coming along, slow but sure, and probably would offer for the girl in a month or two, simultaneously restoring sister and niece to respectability. But Charlotte had turned purple when he'd ventured his opinion, and he had wisely refrained from arguing with her.

Now here was the Trevelyan chap, just as amiable as you please, wanting to hear about the old days. So Belcomb went on at some length about his youth, and about the Deverell family, who had been near neighbours.

"Then you knew him well?" Basil pressed, after patiently enduring a long-winded account of a youthful escapade. "Harry, I mean," he responded to Belcomb's befuddled look. "The new viscount."

"Ah, yes, Harry. No. Knew Marcus. Harry was much younger. And it was Maria who was his great friend. In fact—" He hesitated, but the brandy had loosed his tongue, and having a listener was a rare experience. "Well, everyone knows what Maria did. But I maintain to this day that if Harry had been home, he'd have tracked her down and brought her back before she could disgrace herself. He knew her ways, you see."

I believe I do, thought Basil. But aloud he asked, "Do you mean that by this time he was thought dead?"

"No. That was some months after. Harry had gone to sea. No choice, poor lad. Old Deverell never had much to begin with, then ruined himself in one speculation or another. Left Marcus a title and a pile of debts—and the old ruin they were living in." Not unfamiliar with such experiences, Lord Belcomb sighed. But it was not his nature to be dispirited, and he became hearty again in a moment. "But that was all before, eh? For they say Harry comes back quite the nabob." And what with contemplating Harry Deverell's new wealth, and the repairs he might make to the family ruin, the viscount whiled away another half hour in Mr Trevelyan's amiable company.

7

Lord Hartleigh, who had begun the day feeling inordinately pleased with himself, was now out of sorts and cross with the world in general. As he gazed down at his attractive companion, he wondered how this picture business had grown so dull and stupid. He barely managed to squelch a sigh of exasperation as Veronica returned his glance with a simpering smile. She was pleased to see that her new bonnet had rendered the earl quite wistful.

For you see, it had been found, at the very last minute, that no other suitable companion could be spared, all the servants being required at home and the rest of the family otherwise engaged. And though it wasn't quite proper for Veronica to be going about with a gentleman before she'd been introduced to society, it was determined by Lady Belcomb to be the lesser of two evils. Thus Lord Hartleigh found himself expounding the merits of landscape painting to an empty-headed young miss fresh out of the schoolroom, who understood not three words in twenty and insisted on interpreting it all as flirtation. Isabella, meanwhile, trailed behind with Lucy, whose joy was not to be described. To hold Missbella's hand as that wonderful lady pointed out the beauties of the paintings was to be in heaven.

Not to imply, of course, that the Earl of Hartleigh—who could have bought every last painting in the gallery and still have had enough left over to buy the building in which they were housed with as little concern for his finances as if it were a new neckcloth he were purchasing; whose simple elegance and individual style had been admired by even the great Beau himself; who, moreover, was as highly respected in the very highest political chambers of the kingdom as he was admired in some of the most elegant private chambers of its ladies—to repeat, this is not to imply that the elegant and sophisticated Earl of Hartleigh would have the same notions of paradise as a little girl of seven. Still, it must be owned that he had looked forward to having a certain rather mousy-looking spinster lady on his arm, and to sharing with her his own knowledgeable enthusiasm for these landscapes.

But in vain did the earl endeavour to slow his companion's pace so that Isabella and Lucy might catch up with them. Veronica, bored with the work, hurried him along. She declared that every scene reminded her of the Belcomb country estate, and cross-examined him on the features of his own country home, Hartleigh Hall. Thus Lucy and Isabella remained several pictures behind—too far away to join in the conversation—and the earl found himself brought in less than an hour to the limits of his endurance.

Fearing that in another ten minutes he would throttle his happily innocent interlocutress, he begged that they might wait for the others to catch up. "Lucy cannot walk as fast as we," he explained to a blankly smiling Veronica, "and I am sure by now she has quite exhausted your cousin with her questions."

"Oh, Isabella doesn't mind," Veronica replied with a giggle. "Your ward is ever so sweet; and look—we're just coming to the landscapes you spoke of."

He, however, was not to be rushed again. He stopped and turned round—in time to see his cousin walking quickly toward Isabella. Blast, he thought. Must the man be forever hovering about?

But Basil stopped only for a moment. He chucked Lucy under the chin, laughed at her grimace, then slipped a note into Isabella's hand . . . and continued in his cousin's direction. A polite greeting to Lord Hartleigh, a handsome bow to Veronica, and Basil was gone, as quickly and quietly as he had come. Isabella stared after him, dumbfounded, then, collecting herself, hastily crushed the note into her reticule and endeavoured to continue her slow progress with Lucy.

Veronica, who had not seen the note change hands, batted her eyelashes, fluttered and smiled and sighed in vain. Lord Hartleigh had seen all and burned with outrage. Not jealousy, certainly. Just the . . . the . . . *impropriety!* A note? What nature of communication was it that could not be done publicly, aloud? His thirty-five years of aristocratic breeding, his faultless courtesy ebbed away, and his mouth tightened into a fine line as Isabella and Lucy approached.

Hoping he had not seen, yet with the sinking suspicion that he had, Isabella met his eyes only for an instant before dropping her own. She glared down at her reticule and its criminal contents, and quickly looked away again—at nothing in particular. "I'm so sorry we've dawdled," she said, too brightly, "but I have as much to learn here as Lucy. I wish I had one hundredth the skill and sensibility evident in even the least of these. Ah," she added, as her nervous glance took in the next series of works, "and here are Mr Constable's landscapes. He sees," she noted, forcing herself to speak to the earl, "what others do not, I think."

"You must not underestimate your own abilities, Miss Latham," he replied coldly, "for most of these gentlemen must get their living by painting, and must concentrate *all* their energies upon refining their skills in the one task. You and I—and your cousin," he added as an afterthought, "are blessed by fortune. We may turn from one interest to the next, all the while knowing we'll be well fed and housed. We who are not forced to one vocation are subject to innumerable distractions. Even in a gallery, our attention is not solely given to *art.*"

The emphasis of these last words left no doubt that he had indeed seen. Isabella felt that the note she carried was like a burning coal which any moment would set her reticule ablaze, proclaiming her disgrace to the world. What must he think of her? But for all her guilty embarrassment, she was angry with him. So quick to judge, so quick to disapprove. Just as he'd been that day at Madame Vernisse's.

"I declare you're right, My Lord," said Veronica, smiling sweetly up at him. "When I look at paintings, they always seem to put me in mind of something else." She turned to her cousin. "Isn't it so, Bella? Isn't that funny cloud just the exact shade of my favorite bonnet?"

"Why, so it is," Isabella replied, wishing her cheeks did not feel so hot. "But we must not say so before Lord Hartleigh, lest he judge us hopelessly frivolous." She felt a tiny hand press hers a little tighter, and looked down to meet Lucy's concerned gaze. The child had sensed her discomfort, had recognised the familiar disapproving look on her guardian's face. She squeezed Isabella's hand again, in sympathy, and Isabella returned the gesture with a smile.

This silent exchange did not go unnoticed by the earl, who muttered something inane about an unfrivolous world being a very dull place, then turned abruptly to continue his progress with Veronica.

It was damned irritating. Yesterday this had seemed a thoroughly reasonable way to spend the afternoon. He'd hoped that spending time with Miss Latham would bolster his ward's spirits. Perhaps it would help him penetrate the barrier between himself and the child. And at the same time, he would spend a few hours in the company of an intelligent young woman with whom he might have a rational discussion about art. But see what had happened. Miss Latham was exchanging secret messages with his disreputable cousin, and his ward had sided with Miss Latham against her guardian. And for consolation, he had a simpering young miss whose reaction to works of art was that they put her in mind of *bonnets.*

They had not gone more than a few paces when they met the youngest Miss Stirewell, whom Veronica greeted warmly. Her display of affection might have been attributed to a deep and abiding friendship, but since the two girls had met only once before, a few weeks ago, the young lady's warmth more likely had other sources. Miss Stirewell's brother, for instance. That worthy eldest son of a baronet was as yet unmarried, and possessed an independent income which would double at his father's decease. Thus, while Veronica would vastly prefer being a countess, she was level-headed enough not to put all her eggs in one basket. In short, when Miss Stirewell offered to introduce Veronica to her mama and brother, waiting in the hall beyond, that young lady agreed with alacrity, leaving Lord Hartleigh, Miss Latham, and Lucy to amuse themselves.

Isabella endeavoured to fill the awkward silence which followed by retying a ribbon that had come loose from Lucy's hair. As Miss Latham bent to the task, Lucy told her, "I hope Uncle Basil doesn't come back."

"No?" said Isabella, forcing a smile. "And why is that?"

"He teases me and calls me Moppet." The hazel eyes met hers. "And he makes Uncle Edward cross."

Uncle Edward was about to utter a mild rebuke when he caught the expression on Miss Latham's face, which exactly matched that of his ward. Both looked as though they were expecting a scolding. A smile cracked his stern features, and he bent down to lift Lucy into his arms.

"I'm certainly not cross with *you*, Lucy," he told her.

She placed her arm about his neck, but pulled back a bit to stare into his face. "You're not?"

"No."

She considered this a moment, glanced at Isabella, then back at her guardian, and asked, "Are you cross with Missbella?"

His ears reddened, and "Missbella's" cheeks, in sympathy, did likewise.

"No, I'm not," Lord Hartleigh replied, although that infernal constriction, which had suddenly seized his chest again, made it difficult to get the words out.

"Good." The little girl surprised him with a shy hug.

"But you may be cross with Uncle Basil," she added magnanimously, "because he *does* tease me, and I don't like it."

"Well, then, we must tell him to stop," her guardian agreed.

Isabella was struck by the way the man's face softened as he held the little girl. She wondered if this was the first time the child had demonstrated any affection for him, for he seemed so surprised and pleased at that gentle little hug. It gave her a queer tiny ache to watch them.

"But here is Miss Latham waiting patiently through these family affairs. Shall we continue our tour?"

Miss Latham acquiescing, he put Lucy down. The child placed herself between them, taking each by the hand. "We'll go on this way," she announced. "It's much better."

They had nearly half an hour to themselves before Veronica reappeared, and despite still feeling piqued about the scrap of paper hidden in Miss Latham's reticule, Lord Hartleigh was beginning to enjoy himself. With the barrier between his ward and himself crumbling, he relaxed, and soon found himself telling of an episode from his childhood, a story called to mind by one of the landscapes.

He'd had a pet frog, which was kept hidden in a box under his bed. His parents had given a party, to which all the best families in the county had been invited. "At the height of the festivities, the frog escaped from its box, hopped along down the stairs and into the drawing room. The horror of the scene was not to be imagined—ladies screaming and fainting; footmen scurrying about, endeavouring to capture the poor creature, and stumbling over swooning ladies."

A giggle from his ward and a low chuckle from Miss Latham encouraged him to go on.

"I awoke, hearing the shrieks, and immediately knew what had happened. I rushed downstairs in my nightclothes, clutching the box to my chest and screaming, 'Eliot! Eliot!' "

Picturing the scene, Isabella could control herself no

longer. She burst into laughter. "Eliot?" she choked. "That was its name?"

"*His* name," the earl gravely corrected. As he went on with his story, he found himself embellishing the tale, just to draw more of that delicious laughter. By the time he had done, she was gasping for breath.

"A true scene of Gothic horror," she told him when she finally regained control of herself.

"It was indeed," he agreed, chuckling. "I defy even Mrs Radcliffe to match it."

"Ah, Mrs Radcliffe!" said Isabella. "Now that is another matter. Do you know, I suspect—"

But he was not to learn her suspicions, for Veronica had returned to them, chattering effusively about dear Miss Stirewell and her charming mama. And as it was drawing near the time they'd promised to be home, they hurried through the rest of the exhibit and out to the earl's waiting carriage.

"By the way, Maria, heard anything from Deverell?" Lord Belcomb had wandered into the small saloon. The house was in its usual state of uproar, with servants scurrying to and fro, moving furniture and bric-a-brac, and he was seeking refuge as distant from his wife as possible. Fortunately, she was engaged in haranguing the chef, and only his sister occupied the room. He didn't hear Maria's quick intake of breath at his question, and when he took a chair opposite, the blue-green eyes met his composedly.

"Harry, you know. Back from the drowned. The new viscount," Lord Belcomb prodded, wondering how the deuce Maria had grown so slow over the years. She used to be such a clever girl.

"Oh. Harry. No. I can't think why I should," Maria drawled. "His own family has heard little enough." Absently picking a stray thread from her sleeve, she asked, in a very bored voice, "What's put you in mind of Harry?"

The viscount described meeting with Basil at his club,

and then, having found another listener (although not nearly as *attentive* as Mr Trevelyan, Maria did listen, more or less—certainly she did not interrupt to harangue him), went on at some length, reminiscing about old times. It was only when he saw his sister yawn for the eighth time that Lord Belcomb left off.

"How very interesting" was her polite response. "And now, if you'll excuse me, Thomas, I believe I must have a nap."

"You're not ailing, are you, Maria? For now I look at you, you seem not quite . . . quite . . . in colour, if you know what I mean."

"Yes, my dear. My constitution hasn't yet adjusted to the stimulation of city life." And, giving him a wan smile, she got up and drifted wearily from the room.

8

Isabella was just removing Basil's note from her reticule when she heard a scratching at the door. Quickly, she replaced the note, and looked up to see Alicia gazing at her from the doorway. "Well, come in, dear," Isabella told her, a bit impatiently.

"Oh, Bella, the most dreadful thing has happened while you were gone." Alicia rushed forward, took her cousin's hand and squeezed it sympathetically.

"What? What?" her cousin returned, alarmed. "Is Mama ill?"

"No, not dreadful like that. But bad enough. Lady Belcomb was at your Mama for an hour this afternoon."

"Well, she's always at somebody—"

"But your Mama *raised her voice*" was the ominous reply.

"Mama?" Mama was not capable of raising her voice.

"It's true. And it was all because of that old cat, Lady Jersey, who wouldn't give me a voucher to Almack's because Mama's grandfather kept an inn."

"I do not understand what your great-grandfather—"

"Not him. Lady Jersey. She told your aunt that everyone believes you are having a love affair with Mr Trevelyan."

"Alicia!"

The girl had the decency to blush, but went on nonetheless, "Well, one does know of these things, so I don't know why I'm not to speak of them."

"Because it isn't ladylike" was Isabella's stern response. But in a moment she softened again, for her cousin looked at her with such concern. "But who or what has put such a scurrilous rumour abroad?"

"From what I could hear—and I did try not to eavesdrop, Isabella, but as I said, even your mama raised her voice . . . anyway, it is apparently because of the way he behaves toward you."

"But it is all play-acting!"

"Lady Jersey and her friends don't see it that way." Alicia went on to explain that added to everyone's observation of attentions considered over-warm even in one's betrothed, there was a tide of rumours of clandestine meetings and a series of bets at White's regarding "a certain cit's daughter." In short, the gossip cast grave doubts on Isabella's virtue.

When her cousin had finished speaking, Isabella did not immediately reply, but sat as one stunned. No wonder Lady Jersey had sent such sly glances her way. And here Isabella had thought it was all on account of that old scandal about Mama. She had not expected to find complete acceptance among the ton—certainly not by the highest sticklers—but to have her name blackened because of the theatrics of an insolvent rakeshame; it was too much! Looking up, she saw that Alicia's eyes were filled with tears. "But darling, it's just ugly gossip," Isabella told her, forcing her voice to be soothing when what she wanted to do was scream and break furniture.

"That's what your mother told Lady Belcomb, but she answered back that our position here was 'delicate enough.' And worse, she said that we would all be shunned on your account." The tears could be restrained no longer, and Isabella found herself spending the next half hour trying to calm her cousin, instead of thinking, which she desperately needed to do. For the first time in her life, Isabella wished she were a man, so that she could have called Mr Trevelyan out, and shot him through the heart. But of course he most likely didn't have one. Well, any organ would do.

But the thought of herself, armed with pistol, meeting

the villain at dawn—and the thorny question of who would have served as her second—restored Isabella's sense of humour. "There, there," she said soothingly. "Aunt Charlotte has a tendency to see the black side of everything. No one will be shunned. We will simply have to set Mr Trevelyan right."

"But she said he would have to marry you, even though your mama said she didn't think you cared to." The innocent green eyes gazed seriously into Isabella's.

"Yes, I can see how that would be convenient for several parties. But Mama is right. I am not in a marrying mood this week, cousin."

Pretending a confidence she did not feel, Isabella was eventually able to persuade her cousin to dry her tears and wash her face and go away and leave her to think.

As soon as Alicia had departed, Isabella retrieved Basil's note, carried it to her desk, and opened it.

> *My dear Miss Latham,*
> *I will not say the other thing, for it so offends your sensibilities, and though I am dreadful, I am not so dreadful as all that.*
> *I apologise for distressing you yesterday—and yet somehow I cannot bring myself to apologise for what I did. Temptation was put in my way, and, never having any pretensions to sainthood, I succumbed. And yet I truly meant you no dishonour; quite the opposite. I am fully prepared to confess my transgression to your uncle, and to offer for your hand. . . .*

At this last, a great wave of anger flooded through her. She crumpled the note and hurled it across the room. Offer for her? The nerve of the man! Did he think she'd offer her fortune and person into his keeping to make amends for a mere kiss? Did he think she'd jump at the chance to salvage her reputation with a hasty marriage? Isabella's bosom heaved in righteous indignation. And when she thought of how he had embarrassed her in front of Lord Hartleigh. . . . No wonder the earl was wont to be so cool to her; he'd probably heard the gossip, too.

Anger carried her through the next few minutes, but it was soon displaced by anxiety. If what Alicia had said was true, Aunt Charlotte would be more than willing to promote the marriage. She could bring considerable pressure to bear—perhaps even through Aunt Pamela. And *she* would make Uncle Henry's life miserable, for he'd never force his niece to marry against her will. This could be quite a tangle, indeed. She retrieved the crumpled letter and carried it back to her desk.

> *. . . I dare not hope that your feelings toward me have changed. I fear, rather, that my behaviour has alienated you entirely. That is why I have not yet attempted to see your uncle. Though I believe that you might acquiesce to the dictates of your family (not to mention those of society), I would rather merit your hand on some warmer basis. . . .*

Isabella felt her cheeks grow hot. Warm indeed—the odious man!

> *. . . It is with the latter hope, then, that I beg you to forgive me and agree to see me again; after all, it was not so grievous a sin I committed. I have some words to utter in my own defence—words which, in all fairness, you must consent at least to hear, and which do not fall easily to paper and ink.*
> *I beg your pardon for the garbled way in which I have scratched down these few sentences. I write in haste, in the hopes of being able to deliver this to you at a time when you cannot refuse it.*
> *I shall be riding in Hyde Park at nine tomorrow morning, and will look for you then.*

She looked up from the flourish of his closing, uncertain

whether to laugh or cry. This was the man her aunt wished her to marry. This fanciful schemer and dreamer who dared to threaten her with a kiss—to be reported dutifully to the head of the family, and paid for with marriage. *He* had transgressed, had set the rumour mills going. He had kissed her, and now he expected to be rewarded with her hand and her fortune.

Under the tutelage of her Uncle Henry Latham, Isabella had learned a great deal about business. He had explained the various ploys and promises which had led her father to near-ruin. Compared to the machinations of men of business, Mr Trevelyan's trick was a child's game. And it would take more than that and an outraged viscountess to bring Isabella Latham to the altar.

Well, I will meet you, you horrid creature, she thought, tearing the note into pieces; if for no other reason than to show how little I care for your pathetic threats—and to put an end to this nonsense, once and for all.

Although the earl was pleased to see his ward so animated, as she eagerly plied him with questions all the way home, he found himself unable to give her his full attention. Over and over, his mind replayed the visit to the gallery, calling up Miss Latham's image and the delectable sound of her laughter as he'd told his frog story. What had possessed him to relate that tale? For a few moments he'd felt young and carefree himself; the painful memories of war, the burden of his responsibilities had vanished briefly, and he was simply a man, entertaining a pleasant young woman. What was there in that? It was only her enticing laughter and its secret, intimate promise that unsettled him.

No, there was more. While somewhat absently replying to Lucy's questions, he found himself wondering if he would have told that story to Lady Honoria. And he wondered why, though that lady possessed every requisite for a satisfactory—nay, superior—wife, he was not drawn to her. She was beautiful, yet he gazed on her with no special pleasure. She was reputedly clever, yet he quickly wearied of her conversation. She was—even Aunt Clem agreed—the best of the lot, and yet, and yet. . . . He shook himself out of his reverie as Lucy's voice became insistent.

"Then *when,* Uncle Edward?"

"What was that, child?"

With an exasperated little sigh, Lucy repeated, "*When* may we see Missbella again?"

"I don't know." When indeed? "Her family is to give a ball in a few days and she'll be quite busy. Perhaps after that. *If* you remember the special task you were to perform for me."

"My special task?" The hazel eyes looked away from his as she concentrated, trying to remember.

"Now you see, Miss Latham has put it quite out of your head. The pony. You were to decide what colour pony we should have."

"Oh yes! I know!" She bounced up and down, excitedly. "A silver one. Like the one in the picture. With the white on his face."

"Ah, well, that's a difficult order—" Then, meeting her look of disappointment, he went on, "Indeed, it is a dangerous mission, you propose, madam, but I, Edward Trevelyan, seventh Earl of Hartleigh, shall undertake it."

Lucy giggled in delight, and rewarded him with a fierce hug.

"Lucy talks of nothing but Miss Latham," Lady Bertram remarked as she poured herself a cup of tea. "She seems almost as much taken with the gel as your cousin is."

The smile on Lord Hartleigh's lips tightened. "I doubt my cousin is taken with much else besides himself."

"You're very hard on Basil."

"He has done little to warrant my compassion."

"Your father was much like Basil, at the same age. Yet he settled down and led a respectable life soon thereafter. Some men come by their sense of responsibility late."

"My father did not manage to squander his entire inheritance in five years—"

"He did not have the opportunity, coming so late to the title, and by then he had a wise and affectionate wife to guide him. But I did not invite you here to quarrel with you, Edward." Lady Bertram, whose back was always straight, straightened it just a bit more, and assumed a dictatorial air. "I wish to know what progress you have made."

The long, strong fingers gripped the wineglass just a bit more tightly. "Progress, Aunt?"

"Don't play the fool with me, Edward. You have narrowed down the field to half a dozen, and I hear Lady Honoria Crofton-Ash is leading by a nose. When do you plan to offer for her?"

"Really, Aunt Clem, you make it sound like a race at Ascot."

"Well?"

Curious how, lately, women seemed so often to be putting him at a disadvantage. Aunt Clem, with her cross-examinations concerning his prospective brides; Lady Honoria, with her meaningful smiles and glances which he was quite incapable of returning; Miss Latham, with her intelligent blue eyes and insinuating laughter. . . . Oh no. Not that train of thought again.

The majestic bosom rose and fell as Lady Bertram exhaled a sigh of impatience. "Are you still there, Edward?"

"Sorry, Aunt. I was just considering how to phrase it—"

"It? What? Will you offer for her or not? If you do not plan to do so, then you must cease paying her such particular attention." Her nephew's blank look told her that Lady Honoria little occupied his thoughts, and inquiries regarding other prospective countesses had the same result. His obvious lack of interest in these eligibles, coupled with his unusually passionate hostility at the mention of Basil, led Lady Bertram to put two and two together. Thus, she ceased her cross-examination, and casually turned the topic to his ward. She enquired about the new pony Lucy had been in such a flurry about, and then easily went on to Lucy's infatuation with Miss Latham. Noting that merely mentioning the young lady's name wrought an interesting change in the earl's demeanour, she pressed on.

"I have conversed with her several times," Aunt Clem said innocently, "and have been much impressed with her good sense. She can also be most amusing—once you can get her away from that cat of an aunt of hers. It's no wonder Lucy likes her. In fact, I've thought of inviting her to tea; but it would be so awkward."

Lord Hartleigh raised an eyebrow. Awkwardness, he knew, was not in his aunt's repertoire. "How so, Aunt?"

"Well, if Lucy is to come, I must have you, I suppose, for I will not have that ninny Miss Carter. And then of course I can't have Basil. But if I don't invite Basil, he'll be horribly put out, for he is quite besotted with Miss Latham."

"The devil he is!" the earl burst out, and then, catching his aunt's inquisitive eye, settled back in his chair and drawled, "I told you, Basil is in love only with his expensive amusements—which, I assume," he went on, unable to help himself, "he would like Miss Latham to pay for. As my father did. As Basil expected me to do. Aunt, you know he has no consideration for anyone but himself, has no thought of responsibility to anyone or anything—"

"In that case, what would you have him do?" his aunt asked. "Unlike you, he has no choice but to marry a woman with a fortune. And if Miss Latham finds him suitable, and is content to have him—"

"What?" Lord Hartleigh sat bolt upright, nearly spilling his sherry in his agitation. "Surely he has not offered for her?"

"Not to my knowledge, but if he should—"

"Aunt, you cannot permit it."

"I have nothing to say in the matter." Calmly, she helped herself to a piece of cake. "I cannot dictate my nephew's behaviour."

"You cannot think to abandon her to his . . . his . . . machinations."

"Edward, I do believe you have a touch of your cousin in you. You are growing quite melodramatic. I am sure Miss Latham is sensible enough to avoid whatever 'machinations' you are imagining. I understand she assisted her uncle and has a surprisingly sophisticated understanding of business. I doubt she'll be taken in easily. And if she is, then we may assume it was because she was inclined to be. May we not?"

Having discovered what she wished to know, Lady Bertram gently turned the conversation to other channels. She noted, however, that Lord Hartleigh never did fully regain his equanimity, and she wondered if he was too much of a fool—as men so often were—to realise what he wanted.

9

Isabella had never sympathised much with her Aunt Pamela's social ambitions. After all, the Lathams were not slave-traders; their businesses were respectable. And certainly they were far better off financially than many of the nobility. The latter were often obliged to bring themselves to the brink of bankruptcy, just to keep up appearances. Look at her uncle, Lord Belcomb.

Had Aunt Pamela not been so ambitious, her four daughters might have had their pick of any number of respectable, though untitled, young men. And Isabella might have stayed quietly in Westford, making herself useful to her uncle, instead of having to spend her time dodging the various parties so eager to make use of her fortune.

But that same social ambition had also provided her current means of escape. Insisting that a proper young lady must be conservant with the art of managing a horse, Aunt Pamela had insisted on riding lessons for her girls. After many debates on the subject, Uncle Henry had finally agreed—on condition that Isabella be taught as well. "The poor child does not have sufficient exercise," he'd told his wife in his quiet but firm way. "She must be encouraged to spend more time out of doors." That his wife demanded too much of the girl within doors was an issue left unspoken, for he had no wish to hear the lengthy denials.

Thus Isabella had been afforded some refuge from the chaos of the viscount's household. And in this one case, at least, the viscountess did not require detailed explanations.

Lady Belcomb's passion for horses, like her need for battalions of servants, had contributed in part to her husband's current unhappy financial state. Isabella, then, had only to don her habit in the morning and take her groom with her, and she would have an hour or more of peace. For that, today, she was doubly thankful.

She had left well before time, both to actually exercise the horse and to clear her own head. She'd lain awake a long time the night before, trying to calculate the risks of flouting her aunt's demands, and had at length determined that if all else failed, she would turn to Uncle Henry. He had straightened out worse tangles. And so, clinging to this comforting thought, she'd fallen asleep at last.

She took a side trail, away from the park proper, where there would be room to run. As she urged her horse to a gallop, the groom, by now inured to her headlong pace, patiently waited. On their first excursion, he'd been convinced the horse had run away with her, and had earned a good-natured scolding for his attempts to rescue her. Today, as he had ever since, he gritted his teeth and fervently prayed that Miss would not be killed—at least not while in his keeping.

But Miss was made of sterner stuff than most people realised. She flew across the meadow, confident and secure. As she felt the fresh morning air and the graceful power of the animal beneath her, aunts and debutantes and suitors faded from her mind. Life made sense again; as it rarely had since she'd come to London. She wished she could continue galloping, on, out of the park, away from the city, and back to her uncle's comfortable home. But one could escape only for moments at a time.

Reluctantly, she made her way back, and was guiding her horse along the more travelled paths (although, at this hour, few travelled them) when she caught sight of Basil. He was still some distance away, and as she watched his approach, she wondered what quirk of fate had led him to her—rather than any one of a hundred other similarly well-fixed young women; and why, like most of that hundred, she could not be content simply to purchase an attractive, well-born husband.

For, though she felt his were no match for the darker good looks of his cousin, there was no doubt he was handsome: slim and graceful, impeccably dressed, with that beautifully sculpted face and those unsettling amber eyes beneath that mane of tawny hair. He was clever and poetic and amusing; he was, in fact, exactly the kind of wickedly romantic hero one might conjure up in one's dreams. But such a hero would want her for herself, not for her fortune. Not, Isabella thought with regret, that a mousy-looking spinster was calculated to inspire passion in any hero's breast.

But Isabella did not realize how un-mousy she appeared at the moment. Her face was flushed with exercise, her eyes sparkled, and her fair silky hair had begun to come loose from its pins. She looked quite . . . fetching. Once again Mr Trevelyan noted that Miss Latham was a great deal more appealing when she was stimulated—whether by merriment, anger, or exercise. It would be a fascinating study to discover the diverse ways in which stimulation might be effected; and more than ever he was determined that such discoveries would not be left to his cousin.

Neither the groom's suspicious stare nor Isabella's cold reply to his greeting disconcerted him. He wished she would look a tad more worried, but there was no help for that. If his speech succeeded, she would no doubt have reason to fret.

"I pray you will be brief, Mr Trevelyan," she told him. "I do not usually ride more than an hour, and I do not wish to cause anxiety at home."

"Briefly, then," he agreed, as they moved on a few steps, out of the groom's earshot. "As I indicated in my note, it is no small matter that I attempted to compromise you—"

He was interrupted by her low chuckle, and an angry light shone briefly in the cat eyes as he asked her to share the joke.

"It will not do, Mr Trevelyan," she told him, her face quickly solemn again. "I am not so missish as to think that a stolen kiss in a public park in broad daylight will sink me entirely beneath reproach."

"I'm afraid you are innocent in the ways of society, Miss Latham."

"No, I've had more than a month's education. If you wish to tattle about that episode, there will be gossip—and it will fuel the gossip you've so carefully cultivated—"

"Cultivated!" For the moment he was taken aback by her blunt assertion.

"Please don't insult my intelligence by denying it. If you truly cared for my reputation, you would not have behaved in a way to excite suspicion. Already half the ton thinks I'm your mistress, for you've shown less discretion in your looks, gestures, and words"—she gave each a special emphasis—"than you would if they were directed to an opera dancer." This being rather a mouthful, she paused for breath, and was pleased to see him look discomfitted. "In short," she went on, "if you do tattle, then you are no gentleman."

Basil had to smile at this, for though it was not what he'd expected, it was an apt rebuttal. Was she nearly a match for him, then? How utterly fascinating. "But perhaps I am not" was his amiable rejoinder.

"That's your lookout," she snapped, "for though you tell tales into the next century, no one can make me marry against my will. And before you think to frighten me with threats of scandal, think on this: My Uncle Henry—not Lord Belcomb—manages my funds. And Henry Latham would never deliver me into the hands of a fortune hunter." Her hands tightened on the reins as she turned her horse, preparing to depart.

"Stay, Miss Latham," he urged, bringing his own mount around to block her retreat. "Those are harsh words, indeed." As she opened her mouth to retort, he held up his hand and continued, "And I don't deny I deserve them.

But before you reject me out of hand, there's one other matter I wish to lay before you."

"I cannot imagine any other—"

"My cousin, you know," he said quietly.

There was that odd flutter near her heart, but she kept her face stony as she met his gaze. "I don't see what Lord Hartleigh has to do with this."

"You don't?" The glitter in his eyes belied the innocence of his tone. "How strange, for *I* do. I see, for example, that you have developed a *tendre* for him—oh, don't trouble to deny it," he continued as he heard her quick intake of breath. "I may be a thoroughly disreputable creature, but I am not an idiot. Even your aunt can see it; and doesn't like it above half, I assure you."

"Your imagination is running away with you," she interjected, but weakly.

"I wish it were. But no, the Fates are all against me. For here is Edward, in love with the fair Lady Honoria, who would make a most suitable mama for Lucy. But Lucy can't abide her. No, Lucy wants Missbella for her mama, and no one else will do. I greatly fear, my darling, that Edward will offer for you, just to please his ward. That he will be spiting me in the bargain will, I assume, add some little zest to the venture."

Of course. Lady Honoria. Had it not been obvious? Yet he'd give her up, for his ward's sake? Isabella's momentary joy at the prospect of being Lord Hartleigh's wife was quickly swamped by a wave of despair. To marry her, out of a completely selfless sense of duty. . . . No, he was not so indulgent a guardian as all that.

Basil felt the tiniest tweak of conscience as he watched the play of emotions on her face. Her confidence was crumbling, and the colour had drained from her cheeks. He sighed. "I suppose it must all come about right in the end. I hope so, for your sake. Imagine what it must be like to be married to the man you love, knowing he gave up the one *he* loved, out of too-acute notions of responsibility.

Wondering," he went on, as though talking to himself, "as Lucy grows into adulthood, marries, goes away—wondering whether he'll come to love you in time. Or whether he'll come more and more to resent you."

It was cruel of him to say it, it was cruel to paint that bleak picture—yet wasn't it *true?* She couldn't deny how precious Lucy was to her guardian, how much her happiness meant to him. Hadn't Isabella seen ample evidence, time and time again? She forced herself to respond. "You presume a great deal," she told Basil, her voice flat and tired. "That Duty would lead your cousin to such a step; or that I would accept. I have no wish, no need, to marry anyone."

"But your family?"

"What of them?"

"Let's be businesslike about this," he said briskly. "In marrying me—or my cousin—you're firmly established in society. With Edward or myself to smooth matters with his family, there will be no difficulties in Freddie's marrying Alicia—if she'll have him. And then, when your other little cousins are ready to join society. . . ." Rebellion gleamed in her eye; abruptly, he changed his tack. "Pray don't look at me as though I were an ogre. I was trying to be practical, pointing out the assets and liabilities—and it doesn't suit me, I'm afraid. But the fact is, I care deeply for you, Isabella—"

"In spite of my fortune," she noted sarcastically.

"I'm cursed with an extravagant nature and little income of my own. I have no choice but to marry a wealthy wife. But that doesn't mean I have no feeling for you. The truth is, I've never cared for anyone so much in my life; except myself," he finished, with a rueful smile.

"Surely you realise I don't return those feelings."

"Not now. But maybe in time. If you'd but give me the chance, I might earn your affection."

Looking down at her hands resting on her saddle, she heard the sincerity of his voice, but missed the flicker of amusement in his eyes. "My uncle has taught me to steer clear of speculation," she answered, softly.

"I promise it is no gamble. I can prove it, but you must give me the chance. Will you at least think on what I've said?"

Oh, indeed she would. No doubt through many long, sleepless nights. She nodded.

"And perhaps we will talk again—soon?"

"Yes."

"And perhaps you'll save me a dance at your cousins' ball?"

"Perhaps." She started to urge her mount away. "I must go home now."

As he watched her leave, Basil shook his head. Pity the girl took it so hard. Well, at least he hadn't needed to bring out the heavy artillery. His recent investigations were all beginning to point in the same direction, but he needed another few days to be sure. And desperate though he was, even he must shrink at blackmail. Fortunately, there *were* other forms of persuasion: It had been well worth losing half a night's sleep to rehearse and perfect his "sincere" speech. Tonight he would compensate for the exertion with a visit to the talented, and very expensive, Celestine.

Henry Latham folded up the letter he'd just finished reading. He removed his spectacles and, taking out a handkerchief, began polishing them, a thoughtful look on his genial countenance.

"News from Alicia?" asked his wife, entering his den with a cup of coffee. She tried to get a glimpse of the letter, which he casually slipped into his pocket.

"No, my love. Business. Appears I'll have to go into town."

Pamela Latham's plump features were eloquent with astonishment. In recent years, her husband had avoided the city at all costs, preferring to send a representative to handle any problems which arose there.

"This matter calls for more than the usual discretion," he explained. "And though I'd trust William with my life, I'll feel more comfortable seeing to it myself."

The cup was placed at his elbow with rather more noise than was absolutely necessary. "You'll not attempt to see Alicia, I hope." Her tone indicated that this was not so much a wish as a command.

"Of course not, my love. Wouldn't dream of it. I'll be there and back in a week—two at most—and they'll never know I stirred from here."

"I fervently hope not, for you know it was a condition—"

"Of course." There was a cold edge to his own voice which told her that the matter was not to be discussed further. So, though she wished for another glimpse of that handwriting, she held her tongue and, like the dutiful wife she was, offered to help her husband pack.

10

While Henry Latham was preparing for his pilgrimage, Lord Hartleigh was already embarked upon one of his own. Like a restless ghost, he wandered from Boodles to Brooks to White's; managed, despite his best efforts, to lose less than a hundred pounds; and failed utterly in his attempts to get drunk. Defeated, he returned to his house shortly after two in the morning, called for his favourite brandy, and retired to his library with a growled command that he was not to be disturbed unless the house caught fire.

Slumped in his favourite chair, without the distraction of his companions, it did not take him long to realise what was wrong. Aunt Clem's confident prediction that Basil would offer for Miss Latham had thrown him into a rage, the likes of which he had not experienced since the day Lucy had been misplaced. Curiously, he had the same feeling of being personally at fault.

At first he'd refused to take it seriously, assuming that if Basil was bold enough to ask, at least the lady was sensible enough to refuse. But the earl's perambulations through the clubs of London had disburdened him of these optimistic notions. A great deal of talk was circulating about the two, and even if only a quarter of it was based on any semblance of fact, Miss Latham's reputation was in an uncertain state. She might be forced to marry Basil, just to stop the wagging tongues.

Benumbed, Lord Hartleigh stared around him at his book collection, at the few choice pictures which adorned the walls of this, his private sanctum. With his intelligence missions ended, he'd turned his energies back to his first loves: literature and art. Lucy's coming had been a further encouragement, for he wanted his ward to grow up with a genuine appreciation of what great minds could create. Lucy would not be like the rest of those white muslin-decked debutantes. She'd be able to talk of and understand something besides bonnets and slippers and shawls. She'd grow into a beautiful, bright young woman, and the man who eventually won her would be worthy of her; not some debt-ridden gallant like Basil, or inarticulate dandy like his friend, Tuttlehope.

Of course, she wasn't old enough yet to share with her guardian his appreciation of books and paintings. In fact, there was virtually no one with whom he could share this love. And from time to time he had wished for such a companion: one with whom he could talk—about Lucy and the many questions he had about raising and educating her and making her happy. About books. About art.

He poured more brandy into his glass. Certainly it was difficult to imagine such conversations with Lady Honoria, or with any of her equally eligible rivals. They preferred talk of fashions, when they weren't flirting or gossiping. As he stared morosely into his glass, his alcohol-laden brain betrayed him, and a pair of intelligent blue eyes seemed to stare back at him. As he remembered those eyes sparkling with suppressed laughter, and a generous mouth parted to deliver a witty sally to one of his remarks, there was a familiar tightening in his chest. Only now he noted that it wasn't an obstruction but an ache.

He remembered the day at the dressmaker's shop, and the way her few gentle words to the child had effectively put him in his place. He remembered his visit the next day, and the way she'd coolly accepted his apologies—and her ghost of a smile when she had remarked that children, unlike the rest of one's possessions, seldom remained where one had last left them. He remembered that first dance, and the way her laughter and good-natured teasing had eased his worry about his ward. And other dances, other conversations; those scattered moments in her company, each so unique, all pointed to a quality he hadn't recognised before. She had a way about her which seemed to put things right. And now, angry and depressed by turns, disoriented with alcohol, he wished she were here, to put it all right again.

At length, weary of these drink-sodden reveries, he stumbled from the library and made his way, slowly and painfully, to his bedroom. Exhausted, he collapsed, fully clothed, onto the bed. But oblivion would not come. He stared at the ceiling, willing himself to think.

It wasn't so bad, after all, as being in a French prison, dying by inches in the filth. And he'd survived that, had he not?—with Robert Warriner's help, of course. Indeed, if all that was worrying him was the prospect of Isabella's being thrown away on his cousin . . . well, he must stop it, then.

He'd been a fool to let matters go this far. But the task of bringing Lucy out of her shell, added to the rigours of attending on now one, then another eligible young lady, had blinded him to what was going on. Only tonight had he heard how Basil supposedly took Miss Latham, unescorted by chaperone, to Vauxhall Gardens . . . and how they'd been surprised in a *tête-à-tête* at one party or another. He'd also heard of the diverse assignations and clandestine meetings which managed to place Miss Latham in half a dozen different locations simultaneously—and of course there was that matter of the note exchanged at the exhibition. That, at least, he could vouch for; but it did not necessarily make Miss Latham guilty. He knew from long experience that Basil had a talent for manipulating circumstances to his own advantage.

Having insinuated himself into the household, it would be child's play for Basil to learn of her comings and goings, and arrange to be in the right place at the right time. Just as it would be easy enough for Basil to "refuse to betray a lady" if someone asked, "Was that not Miss Latham with you at such-and-such a place at such-and-such a time?" And then smile and look in such a way as to confirm the questioner's suspicions. Basil had no principles, no sense of honour—except perhaps at cards—and would have no trouble with his conscience as he wove his meshes about her. And from what Lord Hartleigh had heard, no one in the Belcomb household was looking out for her interests; quite the contrary. Apparently, Lady Belcomb was more eager for the marriage than even Basil was.

Yes, with his own dogged pursuit of a proper mama for Lucy, he'd betrayed Miss Latham to the enemy. He should have gone with his first instincts; that night, when he'd seen Basil hovering over her, he should have warned her—and then done everything in his power to frustrate his cousin of his prey.

Well, there was no undoing what was done. But he might snatch victory from Basil—if only she would cooperate. And therein lay the problem. He could warn her. He could bribe or threaten Basil. But it was very likely things had gone too far for that. To rescue her, he must offer for her himself.

His throat was raw, his head spun, and something furry seemed to have grown on his tongue. Fighting back the nausea, he forced himself to sit up, and poured a glass of water from the pitcher on the nightstand. Doing so, he caught a glimpse of himself in the cheval glass. His curly dark hair was dishevelled, having been cruelly and repeatedly raked with his fingers. His eyes were red, with dark rings around them. A dark shadow of beard had sprouted on his face. What a pretty prospect for a bridegroom, he told his reflexion. Miss Latham's bound to be bowled over at the sight of you; bound to throw herself into your warm—not to say humid—embrace. Must smell like a French dungeon. If that good.

But tomorrow he would be repaired and refreshed. And

tomorrow he'd present himself to her languid mama. And then, to the lady herself. One way or another, by fair means or foul, he'd rescue her from his cousin.

He struggled with his garments and eventually managed to remove most of them before falling onto the bed once more. This time, sleep came to meet him, and as he drifted off, he fervently hoped the lady would consent to be rescued.

He'd been forced to repeat his request three times before the much-harassed butler had finally comprehended that it was *Mrs* Latham he wished to see. And now, as Lord Hartleigh surveyed that delicate creature, gracefully posed among her numerous cushions, he found himself wondering how she'd ever summoned up the energy to bring a child into the world. She seemed to have barely the strength to keep her own heart pumping.

"I assume, My Lord, that you have some matter to discuss? For I'm certain you realise that I never *entertain*." She made it sound as though she were referring to a rigourous calisthenic activity.

He quickly reassured her on that count, remembering to add some compliments as to her very presence being reward enough—or some such nonsense—and was alarmed to hear himself stammering.

"Yes. Quite so. And I trust it is not about horses?"

His Lordship, whose head was not of the best this morning, wondered for a moment if the alcohol had permanently damaged his brain.

She looked past him at the ormolu clock on the mantelpiece. "I find horses tiresome," she explained to the clock.

Dazed, he assured her that he would not mention horses. "It's about your daughter," he added, growing more uncomfortable by the second.

Slowly, her glance drifted back to his face. "Ah."

Now he rather wished she would stare at the clock again, for it was difficult to maintain his poise under her gaze.

Despite that vacant air of hers, he had the sensation that she was measuring him. Forcing himself to meet her eyes, he began his rehearsed speech. "I have come to ask your permission to pay my . . . my addresses to her," he said, faltering. The blue-green eyes continued fixed, almost absently, on his face. "I realise that ours is but a short acquaintance, but in that brief time I've come to regard her with the greatest admiration and esteem. She has a superior understanding—"

"My dear sir," Maria interrupted, "you needn't catalogue her virtues to me. I am her mother, after all, and know all about them. Besides which, I find it thoroughly exhausting to contemplate her accomplishments."

"I only wished to assure you—"

A delicate white hand waved away his protestations. "Pray do not exert yourself on that account. I rarely need to be assured."

He had no idea how to get on with this conversation, and his head was beginning to throb dreadfully. After what seemed like hours of silence (but were actually only seconds), while the lady thoughtfully examined the diamonds on her finger, he managed to ask whether, then, he might suppose he had her approval?

"Why, of course, My Lord," she replied, perfectly calm. "What possible objection could I have to so eminently suitable a young man as yourself?"

"It is very kind of you to say so." Confound the woman! What did she mean by that? He was overcome with a sudden urge to wrap his fingers around her throat and choke her when a soft, low chuckle escaped from that very throat. That sound! So like, and yet not the same at all.

Meeting his bewildered look, Maria chuckled again. "My dear Lord Hartleigh," she began, "pray excuse me. Isabella is right; I am an incorrigible tease. But you see, I cannot help it. And you look so solemn that one would think you were asking permission to commit some grievous crime. In my experience, lovers are wont to look rather more cheerful, perhaps even idiotically so."

The earl turned away from those suddenly intelligent eyes, feeling somehow unmasked. "Perhaps," he replied quietly, "it is because I am not entirely sanguine concerning my prospects." He didn't know why he'd told her, but her soft "I see" reassured him.

"I *do* care for her," he confessed, as though the words were being pried from him, "a great deal. But I did not realise it until very recently."

"Yes. I understand how that can be. But I must tell you frankly, sir, that I wish you'd realised it somewhat sooner. Isabella has always been a clever, sensible girl, but in the past day or so. . . . Ah, well. Time is always the enemy." She looked at him—rather sadly, he thought—but did not enlighten him further. "Nonetheless, I shall wish you success."

As he rose to take his leave, she added, "I'm afraid you'll not find her at home this morning. But we shall see you tonight?"

He nodded.

"Good." And, giving him a graceful white hand, she bid him *adieu*.

11

After one last go-round, to see that all was as it should be, Isabella slipped away to a temporarily isolated corner of what a great deal of money and a great many servants had turned into a ballroom. Her face ached with the effort of smiling, but it was nothing to the aching of her head and heart. Basil's words had done their poisonous task. Yes, of course she'd been discontented at times in London. And she'd been unhappy at times at home. But there had been nothing in her life—not Papa's death, certainly, for he was a stranger to her—to prepare her for this utter misery of spirit.

And of course it was all her own fault. What business had she becoming infatuated with an earl, for heaven's sake? An earl who had—if one simply looked at what was under one's very nose—already found himself an entirely suitable countess, thank you. See, wasn't he smiling appreciatively at one of Lady Honoria's witticisms? She was reputed to be very clever. And certainly, she was the most beautiful woman in the room.

Isabella gave a small sigh, manufactured a benevolent smile, and gazed out over the multitude. For multitude it was, despite Lady Belcomb's ominous predictions. Mrs Drummond Burrell might scold about "carryings-on," and refuse to honour the proceedings with her presence; but the vast majority were not such high sticklers. And they were curious to see for themselves Isabella and Basil in action. For the sad truth was, a great deal more had been talked about than had actually been seen, and London Society was eager to learn whether Isabella would outdo even Caro Lamb in making a public spectacle of herself. To society's disappointment, Miss Latham was the perfect lady, and Mr Trevelyan's behaviour was punctiliously correct.

But Isabella was far less concerned with the ton's interest in herself than with their utter lack of interest in Alicia. The dowagers were coldly polite when they weren't out-right rude, and the debutantes ignored her altogether. That Alicia was wealthy and devastatingly beautiful made her crime—a cit's daughter trying to elbow her way into So-ciety—all the more heinous. Thus the early part of the evening had been an agony for Isabella.

Few gentlemen asked Alicia to dance, and those few were the same indigent gentlemen who'd made up Isabella's ad-miring circle in recent weeks.

Lord Tuttlehope had arrived rather late, on account of changing his clothes fourteen times and ruining two dozen cravats. And when he finally did arrive, he was so mortified at his tardiness and so convinced of having sunk forever in Alicia's esteem on this account that he was afraid to speak to her. It thus took him some time to notice that Veronica was surrounded by admirers and Alicia was not. Gradually, it penetrated his wits that his golden-haired darling was being snubbed. This made him mightily indignant, and he forgot his imagined disgrace as he bravely strode up to her.

Somehow Alicia managed to comprehend and accept his incoherent request for a dance, her face becomingly suf-fused with blushes. These having effectively routed his embarrassment, though causing him the most exquisite pain, he was able to keep both from treading on his fair one's toes and from stumbling over his own.

The next dance was claimed by Lord Hartleigh, who, if truth must be told, would never have noticed Alicia's plight on his own. But more than once he'd noted the concern on Isabella's face and her worried glances toward her attractive cousin. When the dance was over, he lingered a moment longer than necessary, as though he found Alicia's conversation utterly fascinating. The moment was just enough, however, to raise a flutter in the fair Honoria's breast and to kindle the competitive spirit of all the fine gentlemen in the immediate vicinity. After all, Alicia Latham was beautiful and rich, and if the Earl of Hartleigh, with his immaculate breeding, did not object to this cit's daughter, why should they? Within a quarter hour, Alicia found herself forced to break at least a dozen hearts because there were not dances enough to go round or hours enough to go round in.

Lord Tuttlehope, however, for his astounding act of courage, earned the promise of a second dance, and was allowed the unlooked-for privilege of escorting Alicia in to supper. Emboldened by this honour, the baron declared that he personally would speak to Lady Cowper in the matter of obtaining Alicia a voucher for Almack's. "But Lady Jersey has already refused me," Alicia gently reminded him.

"Her own grandfather was a banker. Don't know where she gets her notions. But no one shall refuse *you,*" her hero replied, and blinked so hard at his own audacity that his eyes watered.

Alicia had found a moment to hurriedly relate this interesting exchange to Isabella before an eager young major swept her back to the dance floor. So, Isabella thought, Lord Tuttlehope had a spine after all. But would his family accept his choice? Though they might not be able to influence the young man, they certainly might contrive to make Alicia miserable. Immersed in her own thoughts, Isabella did not hear the two young ladies approach, and as she caught the drift of their conversation, she backed away into the shadows.

"Well, I wondered at it myself, but Lord Hartleigh has unusually high notions of duty. And he has always been the most chivalrous of men. How can one be surprised at his acknowledging the little merchant princess when he's taken in that nameless orphan child?"

"That is true, Honoria. And he thinks the world of the little girl, does he not?"

"Yes" was the tart reply. The rest Isabella did not hear, for the ladies slowly moved on.

Of course. Basil wasn't the only one to see it. "Unusually high notions of duty." She'd wanted to think it was for her own sake he'd asked Alicia to dance, but it had been chivalry, plain and simple. Another maiden in distress, and there was the Earl of Hartleigh, to the rescue.

"Ah. So here you are. I feared you'd gone off with your sketchbook and pencil—for a change, you know."

Still caught in her unhappy meditations, her gaze stuck at the intricate folds of his neckcloth for a moment before she looked up into Lord Hartleigh's face. He was smiling, but there was an intensity she'd never seen before in his dark eyes. Her heart beat a little faster as she forced a smile in return. "I . . . we . . . had not expected such a crush—"

"Yes. This affair is an obvious success. But all the same, the role of hostess can be wearisome."

"You give me too much credit. My aunt is hostess, and more deserving of your sympathy—"

"Your aunt has assumed the rights of office, but it's clear you have its responsibilities; not that you need have any anxieties. Your cousins have obviously taken."

He spoke as though he understood her mind, as though he genuinely cared what she felt. And *he* had been responsible for Alicia's success. The ton respected him. "Yes, My Lord, I think you are right. And I believe I owe you some thanks—"

But he sensed what she was about and wouldn't let her finish. "Your cousins are lovely, and Alicia has a genuine warmth and good nature which is tremendously refreshing. But I did not come to talk of your cousins. I have come for a dance. To command you to dance, if need be, for here you have been having all the responsibility and none of the fun."

She took his proffered arm, wishing she had the willpower to gracefully decline. But of course she could not. The muscular arm was a comfort, as were those warm brown eyes, as was that low, calm voice. While he spoke to her, all the gossip and snobbery receded into a distant background. And now, as they danced, even the bleak picture Basil had painted seemed a little brighter. What if he did love Lady Honoria? Wasn't it better to take whatever crumbs he might offer than to go on suffering as she had since that morning in the park? Even if in time, after they were married (she flushed at the thought), he came to resent her, he would be too much the gentleman ever to show it. But his next words called her back.

"Miss Latham, I hope you're not drifting away to a more interesting place, just now when I most need your help; for Lucy insists that I describe your gown in exact detail to her tomorrow morning. And though I have scrutinised you carefully, and committed you to memory, I fear my ignorance of feminine *couture* will cause me to fall far short of my ward's expectations."

She was brought back to earth with a jolt. And suddenly the accumulated tensions of the last few days were too much for her. She was exhausted. Since that meeting with Basil, she had slept fitfully—when she had slept at all. The ball preparations had demanded her constant attention. Her aunt's nagging had been a constant strain. Alicia's difficulties at the start of the evening had stretched her nerves taut. And now this innocent reminder of why he sought her out, why he was so kind to her, undid her. She tried to inject humour into her voice as she began to explain Madame Vernisse's mysteries, but her voice faltered, and tears glistened in the corners of her eyes.

Lord Hartleigh, who had been more intent on watching her lips and eyes than on listening to her lecture, found himself in a turmoil. His instinct was to take her in his arms and comfort her. But this was a crowded dance floor, and she was the object of considerable speculation as it was, and, well, it just wasn't done, no matter how one longed to do it. He willed himself to speak calmly as he asked, "Miss Latham, have I said something to distress you?"

"No." She wouldn't meet his eyes. "No, of course not. But I believe that between the crush of the people and the heat of the candles—"

"Yes, of course," he interrupted. "We must find you a quiet spot and a cool drink." Calmly, he led her away from the dancing, gracefully discouraging the several guests who attempted to stop their progress with chatter. As they reached the doors to the hall, he asked, "Shall I send one of your cousins to you? Or your mother?"

She smiled up at him, grateful for his thoughtfulness, even though it made her ache all the more. Of course it wouldn't do to wander off alone with him. Not in the circumstances. "My mother, please. To the small parlour."

He nodded and was gone in search of Maria. But Mrs Latham was much too fatigued to leave her comfortable chair. "Pray, bring the child a glass of lemonade," she drawled. "Isabella has a frighteningly strong constitution, and I'm sure will recover completely in a very few minutes." Seeing his hesitation, she added, "It's obviously the heat of the room. I'm sure she can be safely entrusted to your care for *five or ten minutes,* Lord Hartleigh. And if she's not recovered by then, I shall send a servant to attend her to her room."

"Five or ten minutes?" Was she telling him to take advantage of the opportunity? It was absurd, yet he hurried to procure the glass of lemonade. His practised calm served him well as he hastened, without appearing to do so, from one room to another, seeking this mysterious "small parlour."

At length he saw the slender form in the gown of sapphire-blue silk he'd studied so carefully. The room was crowded with the excess furniture and bric-a-brac which had been moved out of the rooms in which the festivities were taking place. She was standing by the window, her back to him. One silky blonde tendril had slipped from its pins to caress the soft white skin of her neck, and he found himself wanting to plant his lips on the spot. Instead, he gently touched her shoulder. She started, and when she turned, he saw the tears in her eyes. "My m-mother?" she gulped, looking past him to where there was . . . nobody. And then, hastily, she wiped her eyes.

There was that great treacherous ache again. He deposited the lemonade on the nearest horizontal surface and took her into his arms. It was instinctive. He meant only to hold her, comfort her, but when she raised her head to speak, he saw the slight tremor of her lips, and could not keep his own from touching them. And that, too, suddenly wasn't enough. Her mouth was so soft, so warm. A faint scent of lavender seemed to tease him closer. His arms, of their own accord, tightened around her, and his lips pressed hers, gently at first, and then, as he felt her hands creep up around his neck, with increasing urgency. His pulse raced at her touch, and for a few delicious moments, as she responded to his kiss, he gave himself up to desire. The warmth of her slim body, its surprisingly sensuous curves molding to the hard muscle of his own, sent his blood rushing through his veins. He could feel her heart beating in the same wild rhythm as his own, and his lips moved from hers to draw a trail of kisses along her neck . . . to her shoulders . . . to the creamy flesh swelling at the neckline of her gown . . . and then she began to pull away. He wanted to lift her in his arms and carry her away—to . . . to . . . good God, what was the matter with him?

Summoning all his willpower, while inwardly cursing the place, the circumstances, all the rules and duties that made it impossible to take her now and make love to her, he released her. "Forgive me," he whispered as she backed away.

"Yes. Yes, of course. These things . . . happen."

Her voice was calm, detached, yet her lips trembled, and he ached to kiss them again. But it wasn't right. And there was so little time. Twisted one way by guilt and the other by the passion she'd so quickly, so surprisingly aroused, he found it impossible to gather his wits, and his words came out in a confused rush. "It isn't what you think—that is, I don't know what you think—but I didn't mean to distress you. I couldn't help—Isabella, I want you to be my wife."

The blue eyes which met his for an instant were filled with longing—and sadness—but when she quickly looked away again, he wasn't sure that he hadn't imagined it.

"That really isn't necessary, My Lord. After all," she added ruefully, "I didn't offer much of a struggle. None, in fact. Which makes me equally to blame."

"Blame?" he repeated, taking her hand. "When you've given me a glimmer of hope?"

The colour deepened in her face. "Please—we must end this . . . this . . . conversation. My family will be looking for me." She tried to pull her hand free, but he clasped it tighter still.

"Only tell me that you'll consider—"

"I cannot."

"No. Don't say you cannot. I know this is not the right time or place. I know it's too sudden. But I spoke to your mother this morning."

Her head went up in surprise, but he went on, oblivious to all but his urgent need to hear just one hint of encouragement. "Isabella, surely you must realise—you must have recognised by now that I hold you in great regard." Oh, why would the words be so stiff? But it was either that or, confess to a passion which he hadn't suspected until a moment ago. And he'd shocked her badly enough already. Blindly, he plunged on. "And though I can't expect you to return those feelings now, will you not at least allow me the hope of earning your affection? We share so many interests; we're not entirely unsuited. And Lucy, who adores you, would be the happiest girl in the world."

"Please," she begged, "no more."

"You will not let me hope? Have I so disgraced myself?"

"No. It isn't that. But I cannot consider your proposal."

The words chilled him, and he tried to keep the frustration from his voice as he asked. "Is there someone else?"

There was a rustling of silk at the door, and a bored voice enquired, "Are you here yet, Isabella?"

The earl immediately released her hand, and Isabella hurried to her mother's side. "I was just returning, Mama. Lord Hartleigh was kind enough to . . . to. . . ."

"Yes, of course. Well, your aunt is asking for you, my love, in the most insistent way." Maria Latham allowed her daughter to leave, then turned to the earl. "Time, my lord. It is always the enemy, is it not?" Then she, too, was gone.

Isabella retired briefly to her room to compose herself and rinse away the evidence of tears. "Regard." "Shared interests." "Not unsuited." And, of course, Lucy. If there had been but one word of love. No, affection would have been enough. And if he chose to press her, she'd settle for even less. For regard. For tolerance. And that was impossible. Because every one of her senses had responded to his kiss. His kiss. Even now she could not believe she hadn't dreamed that embrace, for it was so like the other dreams that had come to her, unbidden, so many nights.

Gracious God, what had she done? No protest, no faint pretence at distress or disapproval. He had touched her, and she had gone to him, unthinkingly, returned his kiss with a hungry passion which even now swept through her in waves, making her tremble—and making her ashamed. What had driven her to humiliate herself in that way? It was shameful enough that she wanted him so badly, but she, sunk to the very depths of immodesty, had *shown* him she wanted him. And he? He had only wanted a mama for Lucy. But instead he'd found himself with a love-crazed woman in his arms. What choice had he but to politely accept that love?

He'd felt sorry for her—Lucy's prospective

stepmama—and sought only to comfort her. And then, when she had behaved in that shameless way, he'd gallantly blamed himself for her behaviour. It was unbearable. She loved him past all reason, and he . . . he "held her in great regard." To be his wife on those terms was unthinkable.

No, her course was plain. She would accept Basil this very night, for by tomorrow her resolve would weaken again.

She was left to cool her heels for some time, however, for when she returned to the ball, Basil was oblivious to her efforts to catch his eye. He had seen her exit the room and his cousin follow shortly after. He had seen her mother follow some minutes later. The mother had returned, and the cousin had returned, but there was no Isabella for a quarter hour. Things looked promising. If Edward had offered and been accepted, would not the two have returned together, happily? But Edward was looking like a thundercloud, and Isabella's company smile was frozen on her face.

Calmly, Mr Trevelyan returned his plump partner to her chaperone. He then danced with two more antidotes before leisurely making his way to Isabella's side. "Will you dance, Miss Latham?" he asked, his voice coolly formal for the benefit of the curious dowagers nearby, whose conversation had come to a halt at his approach.

Isabella's acceptance was equally cool. It was only after some minutes of Basil's inane chatter that she finally snapped, impatiently, "Enough. I have decided to accept your offer." He began to speak, but she stopped him. There were conditions, which she would discuss with him tomorrow, in private. Meanwhile, she would trust him to say nothing, hint nothing—to anyone. He solemnly assured her of his discretion, but as the dance ended and she rejoined her other company, it was all he could do to keep from shouting his victory to the entire room—and most loudly in the ears of his cousin.

12

It was very late when an exhausted Henry Latham emerged from the elegant town house close by Grosvenor Square. He was not an old man, but the trip to town had been an arduous one. The gentlemen with whom he needed to speak—like his recent host—were reluctant to have their neighbours see him entering or leaving their homes, and thus had set their appointments late into the night. Used to keeping country hours, the businessman found it difficult to keep his eyes open, and his weary feet could barely carry him down the steps. The two figures hovering in the shadows saw him stumble as he plodded down the street, and nudged each other in anticipation: another drunken nob, ripe for plucking.

Well, thought Henry as he made his painful way, it was no surprise that his clients were loath to admit their connexion to trade. He smiled to himself, thinking how many of his host's neighbours were so connected, all trying to hide their guilty secret.

Ah, but it was their way. And their many little hypocrisies had served him well. Honour, pride, the dictates of fashion—their social code was an expensive one. Land was not always profitable, gambling was risky. Thus, sooner or later, a number of society's shining lights found themselves connected with Henry Latham. Whether it was to avoid disgrace and debtors' prison, or merely for profit, these shining lights found themselves working for him. He'd profited from the information these well-placed sources provided, and his sources had shared the profits.

And tonight, he thought, as his weary eyes scanned the empty street for a hackney, his sources had served him well, though there was no profit in it. No, there never was profit in anything his brother had touched . . . but there was still much to do, and he had no way of knowing—yet—if there would be time enough in which to do it. He looked around quickly as he heard in the distance hoofbeats and the rattle of wheels, and then there was an explosion in the back of his head and all went black.

Lady Bertram pounded with her cane on the roof of the carriage, demanding to know why they had stopped. Her coachman's face appeared at the window. "A gennulmun, ma'am," he explained apologetically. "Lyin' in the road. Looks as he's hurt pretty bad."

"Drunk, rather," her ladyship grumbled.

"Beg pardon, ma'am, but 'e don't smell uv hit. 'e's had a hawful whack on the 'ed."

Eager as she was for her bed, she ordered the coachman to investigate. When he reported back that the man was indeed hurt, and that further, the footman had seen two figures scurry off when the carriage approached, she bade the two servants carry the man into the carriage. "We're nearly home," said the countess. "No point in waking up another household. We'll take him back with us and send for a doctor."

As they entered the house, she was surprised to see her nephew, who was just handing his hat and walking stick to a servant.

"Good evening, Edward," she said, then turned her back on him and began issuing commands to the sleepy household. One servant was sent for the physician. Two were sent out to assist in carrying the man into the house. Maids were ordered to fetch tea, brandy, towels, and hot water. Not until the entire house was abustle did she condescend to explain the situation to her bewildered relative.

Lady Bertram brushed aside her new houseguest's

thanks. "I did not wish to disturb you," she told him, "but thought perhaps you'd like to have a message sent to your family."

"Thank you, My Lady, but it's unnecessary. My family is in Westford, and there's no one here in town expecting me at any particular time."

"Well then, as no one will be made anxious about your absence, we won't worry them needlessly. The doctor says you will recover nicely; all you want is rest and proper food. So I will start by leaving you to your rest, Mr. . . ."

"Latham, My Lady. Henry Latham." Seeing her start at the name, he asked, "Is anything wrong?"

Lady Bertram smiled, "Why, no, Mr Latham. Not in the least. But I believe we have some mutual friends." She advanced upon the bed to offer her hand to the astonished patient, and surprised him further by adding, with a chuckle, "And may I say how *very* pleased I am to make your acquaintance."

Not long afterward, she and her nephew sat sipping sherry before a comfortable fire. Lady Bertram did not see fit to enlighten him as to the visitor's identity. At any rate, Edward did not seem particularly interested; not that this came as any surprise. She had seen all that Basil had seen, and a little more. She had, for instance, seen the gloating triumph on Basil's face after he'd danced with Isabella Latham. Miss Latham had looked very unhappy, though she had made a valiant effort not to appear so. And Edward's face had been a mask—cold, correct. But, like Basil, she'd recognised the anger behind it.

Right now he looked as he had when he was a boy, come to Aunt Clem to confide an unhappiness—and, just as when he was a boy, angry with himself for needing to. She knew it was best not to question him but, rather, to let him take his own time and way of getting to it. Still, it was late, and she was no young deb, and she wished he'd get on with it.

In response to her soliciting his opinion of the two young

ladies who'd this evening made their debut, he went on at some length about the little golden-haired one. Then, abruptly, he stopped midsentence to stare at the fire.

"Are you asleep, Edward?" his aunt prodded. "For if you are, I should prefer you continued it elsewhere."

The dark eyes flickered in her direction briefly, then returned to the fire. "No, Aunt, I was just wondering. How badly dipped do you think my cousin is?"

"What difference does it make? You've made it plain you're not in the least concerned for his welfare."

"It's not *his* welfare I'm thinking about. As you well know. Aunt Clem sees all, knows all."

"You make me sound like one of those swarthy gypsy women."

"Then tell me my fortune." His voice was quiet enough, calm enough, but the flickering firelight emphasised the lines of his face, underlining the effort with which he controlled himself. "She won't have me."

"I believe you mean Miss Latham," said his aunt. "She has refused you?"

He nodded, not trusting himself to speak for the moment, for his aunt's words recalled the cramped room and the small detached voice saying, "I cannot," and the frustration seemed about to choke him. He could still taste her lips, still feel the press of her body against his, and it still sent shock waves through him.

He had come to his aunt's house not knowing where else to go, unable to bear the thought of his own pillow, where the remembrance would, he knew, come to torment him. And tomorrow, how would he tell Lucy—for she must be told sometime—that Missbella would never be her new mama?

"You must tell me what happened." As he began to protest, she waved him away. "Don't tell me what a gentleman does and doesn't do, Edward. I know all about it—and you know I don't intend to make this the latest *on-dit*."

"I know all that, Aunt. But there's no point in discussing

it. She made herself quite plain. And though she did not say so, I suspect you were right; she does mean to have Basil." He spat out the name as though it were a curse. The thought of Basil touching her, holding her—it did not bear thinking of—and yet it seemed he'd be doomed to think of it the rest of his natural life.

"You are quite maudlin," she replied, motioning for him to refill her glass. As he did so, she continued. "I cannot believe you are willing to give up so easily after one skirmish. You've been mooning after the gel since you first clapped eyes on her—"

" 'Mooning'!" In his indignation at this lowering assessment of a thirty-five-year-old Peer and former intelligence officer, the earl nearly spilled his drink. "Really, Aunt—"

"Yes, mooning. Ever since she gave you that set-down you so richly deserved, you've been making excuses to see her. Lucy has been a convenient excuse, but I'm tired of it. The sooner you admit that you're head over heels in love with Isabella Latham, the sooner we can talk sensibly. And perhaps find a way out of this coil. I shall never to my dying day understand how you managed to make such a mull of this, Edward. Even an idiot can see how well you suit. But then, men are such blockheads where women are concerned."

Being lumped together with every other male of the species did little to lighten the earl's mood, but he was forced to recognise the truth in his aunt's words. And somehow, even this scolding, though not at all agreeable to one's dignity, brought some small measure of relief, as Aunt Clem's scoldings always did.

And so he found himself telling her all that had happened. When he referred to "forcing his attentions," he was further relieved to hear his aunt pooh-pooh the idea. "You are being melodramatic," she insisted. "She did not scream, or faint, or box your ears. She was even honest enough to admit her own willing participation. And you think she has taken you in disgust?"

"Whatever it was, she refused to even consider marrying me."

"She said she *could* not."

"Will not, cannot. What difference does it make?" he retorted, pacing the floor now. "The answer is still No. And she will marry Basil—"

"That is very likely, unless you prevent it."

He protested that this was exactly what he'd tried to do.

"From what you've told me," said his aunt, taking the tone one would with a particularly slow child, "you did make an attempt. But your strategy was not well considered. And I am very surprised. For though Basil is a clever fellow, he is not nearly as clever as that little Corsican soldier you outwitted—"

"With some small assistance from Robert Warriner—not to mention the combined allied armies—"

She ignored him. "You did not study your opponent, master his weaknesses, or make any attempt to understand his plans. I know Miss Latham has a good head on her shoulders, but I doubt she's come up against one of Basil's ilk before. Don't mistake me, Edward. I love Basil dearly, with all his faults, but even I must admit that he is a very adept liar. So adept that he convinces even himself. Well, after all, his survival has depended upon it. What a great pity he has not entered politics. *Will* you stop pacing, Edward. A body can't think."

Obediently, Lord Hartleigh stopped, and flung his long form into a chair. It was amazing, his aunt thought, that for all his internal distress, only his hair—raked into disordered curls—gave any evidence.

"You're telling me to try again?" he asked.

"Yes. But for heaven's sake, do use a little more guile. I can't believe that when she drew away from you, you didn't think to draw her back with soft words. Instead you make her a speech. One would think you a schoolboy fresh down from Oxford and still wet behind the ears." Lady Bertram gave an exasperated sigh. "What *is* this generation coming to?"

In spite of himself, he smiled. For his aunt was right. He'd been so busy protecting his pride—ashamed of the way his senses had betrayed him, ashamed of taking advantage of Isabella's distraught state—and so busy convincing himself he was protecting *her,* that he'd omitted the most important words; the "soft words" his aunt spoke of. *Regard, respect, suitability*—how cold and patronizing those terms seemed now, unaccompanied by any whisper of affection or love. To one of Isabella's intelligence, how pompous he must have sounded. What an ass he'd been! He looked up to find his aunt watching him, her own face a document of concern.

"Yes, Aunt," he admitted, "I've been a great blockhead. Your perspicacity will never cease to astound me." He lifted his glass in salute.

"I'm merely old," the lady replied, "and have had time to learn." But she lifted her glass in return.

Light was breaking as Lord Hartleigh left his aunt's house. He'd had little sleep in the past three days, but his step was lighter than it had been. He had some hope. Perhaps the odds were with Basil. Perhaps his cousin had won the skirmish and was now on his way to winning the war. But Edward Trevelyan, seventh Earl of Hartleigh, would not relinquish the battlefield just yet.

13

The other members of the Belcomb household were yet abed when the groggy servant showed Basil into the library where Isabella was waiting. Mr Trevelyan himself had slept quite soundly, thank you, happy anticipation serving in his case as a soporific. And though it was an inhumane hour of the morning, he had no complaints. One must expect to make some sacrifices, after all. He was thus at his most sprightly as he entered the room, exclaiming, "Miss Latham, how perfectly charming you look this morning. I would say green is your colour, but then last night I was convinced *blue* was your colour, for you put your cousins altogether in the shade and quite took my breath away. But this morning I am breathless again. I declare it is a privilege and an honour for that dress to be draped upon your delightful person. Exactly as I should like to be," he added, *sotto voce.*

"Gracious God," she cried, "Was there ever such a chatterbox?"

"My love, if I don't talk, then I must *do* something. And at present, what it is in my mind to do would probably not meet with your approval." When he made as if to move toward her, she backed away behind the great desk. He smiled, perched himself on the edge of the desk, and folded his arms. "But I shall endeavour to restrain myself—for the moment."

"Yes," she faltered. "We . . . we have business to discuss."

"How cruel you are. Not business, darling. A wedding." The amber eyes were wide open and innocent—angelic, even. "We're going to be married. And I hardly slept a wink for thinking of it," he lied. Clearly, *she* had not slept. The dark shadows under her eyes emphasised her pallour.

"Yes," she repeated. "We're going to be married. But as I told you last night, there are some conditions." She looked at him, expecting some protest, but he sat quietly, waiting.

"I believe," she continued, "that I am entering into this . . . this—*business*—with my eyes wide open. However, there are some demonstrations of good faith I require. Not for myself, for I have no illusions about your feelings for me—"

"You know I adore you."

"Cut line, Basil," she snapped. "I wish at least you'd stop insulting my intelligence with this absurd pretence."

"It isn't a pretence. . . ," he began, but, thinking better of it, subsided, contenting himself with looking more angelic than ever.

"The conditions are for my family's sake," she went on, in an odd, dry voice. "First, there is to be an end to the gossip about us—"

"But, my love—"

"You encouraged it. Now you can discourage it. The gossip and the wagers are to stop. Completely. Further, you are to behave toward me with respect. And with discretion. You were able to do so last night, and I'm sure you can continue to do so. At least for two weeks, which is the time limit I've set—though I'm sure you could stop the gossip in as many hours."

His eyes sparkled dangerously, but "Yes, dear" was all he said.

"The fortnight's time limit is as much for your sake as my own. I realise that some of your creditors must be satisfied soon. If at the end of this period you have kept your part of the bargain, I shall immediately set things in train to pay the most pressing of your debts. Most of your creditors, of course, will be more patient when our betrothal is announced."

Her generosity astonished him. He'd expected far more difficult conditions. He'd even come prepared for some blows to his pride. But this wasn't what he expected. It was too simple. Puzzled, he asked if that was all.

"No. That is, yes. As soon as I've settled with your creditors, you may do as you wish: send the announcement to the papers, set the date. Whatever." She shrugged. "I shall marry you when and where you say."

"But for a fortnight," he said, slowly, "no one is to know?"

"I plan to tell my mother immediately, and let her decide when to tell my aunt and uncle. In any case, all will see the advantages of keeping silence meanwhile."

"But, my love, how can I be sure *you'll* not slip away from me between now and then, while I'm hard at work crushing gossip and behaving myself?"

"Slip away?" she echoed. "Where? How? Where you have not hemmed me in, my obligations have. You know as well as I that what I ask is a mere token. To undo the damage done to my reputation, to allow my cousins a fair chance. I ask you this for my family's sake—a small act of good faith. And besides," she added listlessly, "I give you my word that I shall not break this bargain."

He was torn between delight and suspicion. "You exact no other promises—no other conditions?"

She shook her head.

"Isabella, you've made me very happy, but you astonish me."

"Why?"

He slid from his perch and circled round the desk to where she stood. This time she held her ground, even as he placed his hands on her shoulders and gazed into her eyes. "Because you might have offered me a marriage of convenience," he replied.

"You may have that, if you wish."

"I *don't* wish it. But do you?"

She stared at him—or, rather, through him—for a long moment before she answered, softly, "There's enough pretence in this business as it is. Let us at least make an honest effort at this marriage of ours. I will try to be a good wife. I ask in return that you make an honest effort to be a good husband."

"But it's so very unfashionable, my dear."

"Yes. I know it's all the rage to be miserably married and happily unfaithful. Well," she said with a shrug, "you'll do what you like in the end. Only give me some peace of mind for the next fortnight. And now, will you please go away?"

He dropped a kiss on her cheek, and she winced. As he drew away, he found himself, quite unexpectedly, quite angry. But he did not shake her or utter any of the cruel remarks which so quickly leapt to mind. Instead, he manufactured an affectionate smile, and politely took his leave.

Telling Mama was considerably more difficult, for she was exasperatingly obtuse today. At length, when Isabella had outlined the advantages of the match for what seemed the thousandth time, Maria Latham looked down at the diamonds sparkling on her fingers and sighed.

"Will you not at least wish me happy, Mama?" her daughter pleaded, struggling to keep her voice even.

"I cannot wish you happy when you persist in telling me the most outrageous bouncers, my love."

Startled by this accusation, Isabella gave a guilty glance at her mother's face, but Maria went on as though she noticed nothing. "But then, darling, I am quite at your disposal, and prepared to wait all day, if need be, for you to tell me why you have so abruptly decided to marry Mr Trevelyan." In demonstration thereof, Maria leaned back comfortably against her cushions and gazed out the window.

"But, Mama, I've told you several times already."

"Then I suppose you must tell me again."

Minutes ticked by as Isabella considered whether to give up and leave the room. Yes, there was a great deal more she could tell, but she couldn't bring herself to confide in her lackadaisical parent. And perhaps, anyway, it wasn't confidences Mama sought. As it became clear that no guidance was to be volunteered, Isabella asked, "What exactly is it you wish to know? And why did you say just now that I had lied to you?"

"It is equally a lie to me when you leave things out as when you put the wrong things in." The sudden flush on her daughter's face indicating a direct hit, Maria went on, once again apparently taken with what was beyond the window. "You have gone on interminably about Mr Trevelyan, yet you have not even thought to mention why you've refused Lord Hartleigh."

"What has that to do with it?" Isabella burst out before she had time to wonder how her mother knew. Had she been eavesdropping last night?

"That's what I would like to know. For Lord Hartleigh *most properly* sought my permission to pay his addresses to you." (The fact that Mr. Trevelyan had not done so was thus left disapprovingly implied.) "And since last night I provided him with a decent opportunity in which to make a start—"

"Mother!"

"—and came upon you gazing soulfully into each other's eyes—"

"Mother!"

"—I must confess myself at a complete loss as to why you are telling me of your engagement to his *cousin*. It is quite the most ridiculous thing I've ever heard—your aunt's daily conversation excepted, of course."

This was too much for Isabella, who dropped into a chair and promptly burst into tears. Her mother bore this demonstration with perfect equanimity, and at length, when Isabella had regained some measure of self-control, bade her come sit by her and tell the entire story.

This exercise occupied a full half hour and was punctuated with sobs, tears, and an occasional hiccough. When it was done, Maria calmly ordered tea as a restorative.

"My love," she said some time later as she thoughtfully stirred her tea, "this is a bewildering tangle indeed."

Isabella merely nodded. To speak, she thought, was to choke. For now that she'd confessed her infatuation with the earl, every memory she'd so ruthlessly crushed last night and this morning rose up to haunt and torment her, compounding the exhaustion which had already made her dizzy.

"You are quite convinced that Lord Hartleigh's offer was primarily motivated by his ward's desires, rather than his own?"

"Yes" was the dismal reply. "And even it if weren't—which I know it *is*—it's too late now. I've given my word to Basil."

"Yes. Well. You know, Isabella, I do believe my lifelong opposition to arranged marriages was ill considered. It is perfectly amazing what a mull of things the principals will make when left to themselves. And it seems, now I think of it, to run in the family."

Isabella was too caught up in her own misery to perceive the implications of her mother's admission. She simply nodded in agreement.

"Well, at the moment I cannot think what can be done to mend matters. All these complications and insinuations and declarations—I confess it's quite beyond me. At any rate, I don't think it necessary to mention your betrothal to any of the others just yet. For now, we must be content to hope for the best. I shall hope, for instance, that your Intended is struck and killed by a passing carriage. This afternoon, preferably," she murmured, half to herself, "just about teatime. Now *that* would be an aid to the digestion." She got up, absently patted her daughter on the head, and left the room.

A moment later she put her head back through the door. "Which reminds me, darling. I shall be joining Lady Bertram for tea today. She was kind enough to invite us this morning, but I think it would be better if you stayed home with a headache."

It had been an overcast, oppressive day, and the air's heaviness seemed to have cast its pall on the features of the three who sat, pretending to take tea. Mr Latham was embarrassed and uncomfortable. Lady Bertram was never embarrassed, but her dignified features were thoughtfully solemn. Even Maria, who rarely registered any expression but *ennui,* had a tightness about her face which, in her, was indicative of perturbation.

It was the countess who broke the silence, striving to put the usually genial Mr Latham at ease. "No," she told him firmly, "you were quite right in making your investigations. She is your niece, after all. Certainly, I should have done as much, in your place." She lifted a tiny sandwich from the tray, looked at it as though it were a venomous serpent, then dropped it onto her plate and forgot about it as she turned to Maria. "And given the horrifying state of Basil's finances . . . well, in your place, I would have no scruples in forbidding the match, regardless whether she is of age, regardless what foolish promise she made Basil. Unless, of course, you are persuaded that she has conceived a passion for him and will be thoroughly miserable without him. And somehow," she added, with a ghost of a smile, "though he is a devilishly charming wretch, I cannot believe he has managed to charm *her.*"

"No, but he *has* persuaded her," Maria replied.

"But surely you are not prevented by this scandal he threatens you with. If I may be blunt, Maria, you've survived worse."

Maria's features tightened just a bit more as she pondered this for a moment. Then, after casting a swift glance at her brother-in-law—who reddened slightly—she turned to the countess. "The scandal you speak of is nothing. Isabella is naïve to take it so seriously—perhaps because others around her make so fatiguing a fuss about it. But no, that is not the matter. Certain facts have recently come to my brother-in-law's attention—"

"Maria!" her brother-in-law interposed in a low, warning voice.

"Do not trouble yourself, Henry. Lady Bertram is entitled to know. And it is my experience," Maria went on, meeting that lady's gaze unwaveringly, "that she is the soul of discretion."

In a quiet voice, she went on to tell her story, interrupted once or twice by Lady Bertram's expressions of sympathy and surprise. When Maria had finished, the trio sat in silence for several minutes. The tea had grown quite cold by this time, and the biscuits and tiny sandwiches seemed to have hardened into rocks.

"But this is infamous!" Lady Bertram finally exclaimed. "And your daughter knows nothing of it?"

"With Harry presumed dead, there was no reason to tell her. It would only have made her unhappy, needlessly, and forced her to carry my secret as a burden for the rest of her life."

"And now?"

"And now I feel I owe it to Harry to discover *his* wishes in the matter, first."

"He has been wronged enough," Mr Latham put in, "that we wished not—even inadvertently—to wrong him further."

"But why do you tell me this? Surely Harry will not want the tale bruised about, regardless what he wants Isabella to know or not to know—" Lady Bertram stopped suddenly, as a suspicion struck her. "Ah, now I see. Basil. He has somehow ferreted out the truth."

"He has questioned my brother quite closely about Harry Deverell."

"And just last night, My Lady, I learned that he is likely in possession of a letter never intended for public consumption."

120

Lady Bertram shook her head sadly. "Poor Basil. What a dreadful boy he's turned out to be."

"Not so much dreadful, I should think," Henry suggested tactfully, "but careless, as so many young men are. And now, it seems, desperation has soured his better nature."

"That is very generous of you, my good sir, but I know my nephew, and he has been devious since the day he was born. Well, there's no help for it, then. I will have to speak to my man of business—"

Mr Latham jumped up from his seat in agitation. "Gracious Heaven, no, My Lady! It will never do. You'll pay the old debts and he'll go on making new ones. No, no. It is unthinkable." He was adamant, shaking his head even after he'd finished speaking.

"Henry is right," said Maria. "And he has some ideas of his own on how we may proceed. Furthermore, you've forgotten about your other nephew, who—unless I am greatly mistaken—will not be content with Isabella's tiresome excuses."

"He's been devilish slow and thickheaded so far" was the muttered response. "To stand there and take no for an answer when it was plain as the nose on his face . . . but then I told him what I thought." She turned to the gentleman. "Well then, sir," she urged, with the air of a conspirator, "tell us your plan."

14

"Uncle Edward! Look! Look!" But this time, instead of indicating her own accomplishments in the saddle, the child on the silver-grey pony was pointing in the opposite direction, across the meadow where a familiar figure in a dark green riding habit had just emerged from one of the park's side trails. Though she was some distance away, neither Lord Hartleigh nor his ward had any difficulty in recognising Miss Latham.

"Oh, Uncle Edward, it's Missbella. May I show her my new pony?"

The earl was about to agree when he saw Miss Latham turn back angrily toward her groom, then set her spurs to her horse and dart away. "No, I don't think so," he said slowly, never taking his eyes from the slim figure on the brown mare. "She is going rather fast"—he noted with alarm that it was very fast indeed—"and we had better not distract her."

Blast her! John, the groom, cursed to himself, watching helplessly as his mistress galloped across the meadow. Warning him to keep away, she had shot far ahead of him, as if all the fiends of Hell were after her. Was ever a man so cursed to have such a one in his care? Her usual way was bad enough, but at least she was usually in control of herself and her animal. Today, though, she was in a temper, and urged her horse on to a pace that even in a man called for a cool head and complete concentration.

Oh, she was an odd one, no doubt. And not just in her

unladylike riding practices. There was talk in the stables which matched the downstairs talk Polly had passed on to him. And though he made it a practice to believe only half of what he heard, the half that remained did not match what *he'd* seen. Oh, yes, she'd met the light-haired gentleman in the park, but you could look as hard as you liked and precious little sparking you'd see. For Miss Latham might be a plain girl from the country, but she had a will of her own. He swore to himself as her pace increased—for even were she a man, riding astride, it would be a dangerous pace, damn her. She was like that black Arabian his lordship had had to sell at such a loss: quiet on the outside and very obedient, but with a willful streak. Would just take it into his mind he wouldn't have a rider, and he'd just shy and rear up until he was free. Turned around and bit his lordship one day for no reason at all. Aye, the one Miss married—if she married at all—would get himself bit now and then, depend on it.

Lost in earthy fantasies about Miss Latham's relations with some anonymous husband, the groom was slow to react when he first saw the horse shy at a bird that darted past. As John watched in paralyzed horror, the horse abruptly stopped, its head dropped forward, and its rider slipped over its shoulder, tumbling to the ground. Cursing once more his ill luck in having so wrong-headed a female under his care, he whipped his own animal toward the still—too still—form lying in a heap next to the now quiet mare.

But he was beaten to the spot by the Earl of Hartleigh, who was out of the saddle and kneeling beside her while the groom was yet halfway across the meadow. The earl was tearing off his coat as the groom drew near. "Good God, man," he upbraided him, "could you not see that her horse had gotten away from her?"

"B-but, My Lord, that's how she always does—and she won't let me—" The groom stopped, for there was murder in his lordship's eye.

"What's the matter with you, you fool! Can't you see she's hurt? And you there talking? Go for help!"

Relieved to escape the scene of his crime, John dashed away. But even as he rode, tormented with the prospect of losing his place and the even worse prospect of never getting another, he found a moment to wonder why his lordship looked so desperate; sick, almost. It was an odd thing, for one who'd surely seen worse in France and Spain.

Desperate and sick at heart Lord Hartleigh was indeed, as he gently placed his rolled-up coat under her head. He chafed her cold hands, by turns murmuring unintelligible endearments, then muttering curses on himself and his stupidity. Hours seemed to pass thus, rather than the actual few minutes, before her eyes fluttered open to gaze blankly at him.

His heart, which seemed to have stopped from the moment he'd seen her galloping madly across the meadow, resumed some semblance of normal operation. But his voice shook as he spoke her name, and the hand which brushed her fair hair from her face trembled. "Are you all right, Isabella?" he asked softly. "Are you in pain?"

"I never fall," she responded. Her eyes gazed blankly at him.

"Yes, I'm sure you don't," he agreed.

"I never fall," she repeated, more emphatically. As if to prove it, she started to get up, then winced and fell back.

With dismay, he realised that she did not know him or understand what had happened. A sickening dread filled him as he continued to stroke her forehead gently, and tried to make her understand. "You mustn't move. Your groom has gone for help. You mustn't move until we can tell how badly you're hurt."

She insisted that she could not be hurt and that she never fell, and again tried to get up, with the same result. "Stop it," he whispered. "Stop it." He told her who he was, he told her that help was coming soon, but she continued to repeat her two claims, no matter what he said to her.

After what seemed a lifetime, John returned, along with a carriage, a brace of footmen, and a doctor. Reluctantly, the earl gave up his place to the medical man and, only by sheer force of will, restrained himself from throttling that professional as he poked and prodded at Isabella. Turning away in frustration, Lord Hartleigh suddenly remembered his ward. He had barked an order for her to stay where she was when he first took off after Isabella. Had she seen the accident? Or had Tom been clever enough to distract her? Well, there was no time to worry about it now. He called to one of the footmen gawking idly nearby, and sent him off with a message to Tom to take Lucy home. Explanations would have to wait until later.

At length, the physician rose and joined him. The lady, he said, was not seriously hurt, but she was bruised. When the earl hotly argued that she didn't know where she was, he was met with an indulgent smile. "Just a mild concussion, My Lord, but nothing to concern yourself about. A bit dazed right now, but she'll come around in a little while. At any rate, it will be all right to move her."

Rudely thrusting him aside, the earl returned to Isabella and was relieved to find that, though she still didn't seem to know him, she had at least stopped insisting that she never fell. Over the exclamations of the servants, he lifted her in his strong arms and carried her to the waiting carriage. When he took a place beside her and slipped his arm protectively around her shoulders, he met the physician's raised eyebrows. "I have no intention of leaving her to the ministrations of these idiots," the earl growled, his tone daring opposition. "And besides, she should not be jolted overmuch." Well, Dr Farquahar was not a daring man, and decided to keep his opinions to himself.

When they reached the house, Lord Hartleigh insisted upon carrying her up to her room, despite Lady Belcomb's vehement protests that there were strong healthy servants to see to it—and it was most improper—

"Pray control your grief, Charlotte," Mrs Latham interrupted rather sharply. "Your hysteria will not make Isabella the least bit better, and it is very trying to Lord Hartleigh, who, after all, has taken quite good care of her thus far."

Thus silencing her indignant sister-in-law, Maria accompanied Lord Hartleigh and Dr Farquahar to her daughter's room. When the earl had deposited his burden on the bed, he was still unwilling to leave her, but stood instead watching as the doctor mixed a potion of some sort and gave it to his patient. Still apparently oblivious to all that was happening around her, Isabella obediently drank it. After giving further instructions, the doctor left, and Maria turned to her distraught visitor.

"My Lord," she said quietly, touching his arm, "you must come away now."

"I cannot leave her like this," he answered, unable to tear his eyes from the blue ones that looked back but didn't appear to see him at all.

"But you must. When she does come to her senses—and the doctor assures us she will, quite soon—she'll be distressed to find you here." Seeing that her words were having some effect, she teased him gently: "And besides, if you do not leave soon, we must put her to bed in her dirty riding habit—for how can Polly undress her with you there staring, My Lord? That would not be at all the thing, I assure you."

This quickly recalled his sense of propriety, and the earl backed away guiltily from the bed. "Good God," he exclaimed, "what am I thinking of? Madam, you must forgive me—"

"For rescuing my only child? Well, perhaps in time I can manage it. Now come, sir. Let me offer you a brandy, for I'm sure you need it. And you most certainly deserve it." And so saying, she led him from the room.

Basil learned of the accident from Freddie, who had gone to claim Alicia for a drive in the park that afternoon. Upon being informed that Miss Latham was neither dead nor likely to die, Basil coldly remarked that he had not thought she would take such drastic measures to escape him.

Considering that his own heart had been permanently reduced to mush, Lord Tuttlehope was somewhat stunned by his friend's callousness. "Must say, old boy," he chided, "not a joking matter. Didn't know her own mother. And babbled a lot of nonsense at poor Hartleigh—"

" 'Poor Hartleigh'!" Basil exploded. "What the devil has my cousin to do with it?"

"Why, didn't I tell you?"

"Tell me what? All you've told me is that her horse threw her and scattered her wits in the bargain. What has my cousin to do with it?"

"Quite sure I told you," the baron insisted, blinking at this uncharacteristic display of temper.

"You have got your mind stuck, as usual, on something else," Mr Trevelyan noted with some irritation. Then, as he saw the hurt in his friend's eyes, he regained his self-command and apologised. "Sorry, Freddie. I didn't mean to snarl at you that way—"

"Not at all. Not at all." Embarrassed, the baron brushed away the apology. "No need. Worried about the girl, Basil. Know how it is."

No, you don't know how it is, you fool, Basil thought; but he swallowed his exasperation and bore Lord Tuttlehope's inarticulate reassurances with heroic fortitude. Finally, as Freddie sputtered to a close, Basil assembled his features into an appropriately appreciative expression and thanked his friend for his solicitude. "For I know I'm an ungrateful wretch, Freddie. But come, let us have the whole miserable business. I can bear it now." Meeting with two uncomprehending blinks, he prodded, "I believe that, in your anxiety to spare my tender feelings, Lord T, you left out half the story."

And to be sure, he had. When Basil learned the whole of it, he burst into a long and only partially intelligible diatribe on the perfidy of women and the treachery of relatives. Not understanding more than one word in twenty, Freddie listened patiently, but with growing concern. He was used to Basil's extravagant speech, but was not used to seeing him so impassioned. And when his friend had done, he agreed (as he thought) that yes, Basil was barking up the wrong tree. "Best to chuck it," he added, nodding wisely. "Other fish in the sea, Trev."

"Not for me, my friend. Come, let me show you something." Leading his friend to the window, Basil indicated a small, sallow-looking man in the street below. "Solsman and his friends have been very generous, you know, but for a price. I have three annuity payments overdue already and two more in another month. They come by now and then to remind me of our 'little business,' as they put it. But they haven't sent the bailiff for me yet, Freddie. Do you know why?"

Very ill-at-ease, Lord Tuttlehope shook his head.

"Why, they don't want to spoil the wedding plans, my boy. They're really most considerate fellows," he went on as he turned away from the window.

"Didn't know it was so bad, Trev. Only too glad to help—"

"You've thrown enough good money after me, Freddie. But you needn't worry. It's as I just explained to my friend down there on the street. Miss Latham and I have an understanding. A bargain, if you will. And though I'm on my somewhat questionable honour not to disclose the details, I can assure you that it will all come out right. Soon. Quite soon."

He patted his friend on the shoulder and smiled reassuringly at him, but Lord Tuttlehope was not reassured. Long after the baron left his friend's lodgings, he was still trying to understand what had happened, and was still wondering whether it was the moneylenders hovering about like vultures or something very different which had made Basil act so odd.

When he reached home, Lord Hartleigh was relieved to

discover that Lucy had borne the suspense surprisingly well. True, she had refused to be coaxed away from the window where she watched for her guardian's return. But she had waited, dry-eyed and quiet; and, when offered reassurances, had surprised the concerned staff by asserting that of course Missbella was all right—after all, Uncle Edward was taking care of her.

"You're a very brave little woman," he told her as he lifted her in his arms and hugged her.

"Yes," she agreed complacently.

But after he had satisfied her with all the details of Missbella's rescue and happy prospects of recovery, he was a trifle disconcerted to hear his ward read him a lecture. Missbella's family, she maintained, did not take care of her properly, and anyway there were too many of them to look after her as they should. And so it would be best if Missbella came to live with them—for Uncle Edward was big and strong and had only herself to look after. And there was lots of room, wasn't there?

In vain did the earl try to explain that there were rules governing these matters. Lucy informed him that she knew all about it; Miss Carter had told her. Oblivious to her guardian's astonishment, she went on: "Missbella is grown up, and they'll let her go away if she gets married. So you can get married to her and bring her back here and she can be my mama and you can take care of us."

The earl admitted that this was a sensible idea. "However," he added, "it is a very serious decision, Lucy. Whoever Miss Latham marries she will be married to forever. So she must be very, very sure it's me she wishes to marry."

"Oh, she'll be sure," his ward told him confidently. "But you must ask her, mustn't you?"

I already have, he thought. And, recalling the brief conversation he'd had with Maria Latham that morning, he wondered whether it would not be better to discourage Lucy's hopes. "She tells me she has given your cousin her word," Mrs Latham had told him. "And to Isabella, that word is as sacred as it would be to any gentleman. She has had, you see, a rather unusual upbringing."

But Lord Hartleigh couldn't bring himself to disappoint the child, especially after the terrifying experience she'd had, and the courageous way in which she'd dealt with it. So all he told her was that he would speak to Miss Latham, but only after he was certain she was quite well. And though she was fully prepared to assist personally in moving Missbella to her new domicile this very afternoon, Lucy promised to be patient.

15

The doctor's potion had the desired effect, for when Isabella woke in the early evening, she was once again in command of her senses. Her mother, upon determining this, ordered in tea, and spent an hour with her. Because Isabella was still rather dim on what had happened versus what she had dreamed, Maria offered up the account she'd had from Lord Hartleigh. The tale was told in her usual languid fashion, but contained so many sly hints and ironic references to the lengths to which the earl had gone—"solely on his ward's account"—that Isabella was finally moved to plead with her mother, "Stop teasing and tell me plain what you're about, Mama."

"Why, plain then, if you'll have it so, my love," Maria replied, gazing into her teacup as though the story were written there. "A man does not call one *his* 'poor darling' in that anguished tone of voice without some personal concern in the matter." Isabella opened her mouth to argue, but her mother was still talking to the teacup. "Certainly one wouldn't expect him to have rehearsed such words of concern and affection as I heard him whisper at you—although I did try *not* to hear, for it was most improper of him, you know." The cup not deigning to reply, she bent her gaze upon her daughter. "But then, all he did was so monstrous improper that we were all about the ears and didn't know where to look or what to hear. Your aunt, needless to say, was quite beside herself, but oddly enough, she didn't seem to think you compromised by it."

News that a Peer of the Realm has so far forgotten propriety on one's account cannot fail to be gratifying, especially if said Peer is eligible, elegant, and handsome; and,
more especially, if one would rather like to forget proprieties
on *his* account. But the information also made Isabella feel
quite desperate, and for a moment she was sorely tempted
to leap from the bed and hurl herself out the window. If
Lord Hartleigh *did* care for her, then her life was entirely
ruined. It was one thing to give up the man you loved when
he didn't love you. It was altogether another to give him
up when he *did*. It was idiotic, in fact.

As though reading her daughter's mind, Maria went on,
"In light of his behaviour this morning, I find it perfectly
absurd that you have engaged yourself to his *cousin*."

"Oh, Mama, it's not absurd," Isabella cried. "It's completely horrible. Oh, why didn't that horrible animal kick
me in the head and be done with it? What am I going to
do now?"

"Isabella, you are far too unwell to engage in theatrics.
But it's what comes, I imagine, of spending so much time
in Mr Trevelyan's company. Whatever is the matter with
you, my love? You have only to cry off. It's done every
day. Some young ladies do it twice in a morning, I understand. To keep in practice, no doubt." She gazed
thoughtfully at the biscuits on the tray and calmly selected
and nibbled at one while Isabella protested that she could
not. For one, added to her already questionable reputation
would be the label of "jilt." For another, and more important, she had given her *word*.

"Considering that you were deceived into giving that
word," Maria answered, daintly brushing a crumb from
her sleeve, "and considering that your Intended has behaved
dishonourably toward you, I don't think you need feel
obliged to abide by it."

"But, Mama, he's desperate. I know he is. And if I break
my promise . . . I don't know what he'll do."

"You cannot allow your life to be ruled by fear of what

132

he'll do. And what can he do, after all? Blacken your name? Do you think for a moment his cousin would permit it?"

"I don't know."

"Of course you do." Maria stood up. "I would have preferred to postpone this discussion until you were feeling more the thing, but that is not possible. I have often found that in precisely those cases requiring lengthy and calm consideration, circumstances permit neither, but demand instead prompt action. Life can be very trying in that way, Isabella."

It struck Isabella that there was something unusual in her mother's expression. There seemed to be a note of something like regret in her tone, not at all in keeping with her usual air of indifference. But there was nothing to be read in Maria's face. The blue-green eyes were, as usual, focussed elsewhere, and the still-beautiful features appeared untouched by any emotion. She was still Mama, still languid, still an enigma.

"What circumstances do you mean, Mama?"

Maria sighed. "Lord Hartleigh will be here tomorrow. I don't think we need pretend he comes simply to enquire after your health."

"But I can't speak to him yet!" Isabella cried, her pleasure at this message quickly swamped by panic. How could she face him?

"That is both ungrateful and cowardly of you. And if that's the best you can do, then perhaps you and Mr Trevelyan will suit after all." Maria did not wait for a reply, but, in her normal manner, drifted out of the room. Abnormally, however, she slammed the door behind her, making Isabella cringe at the throbbing it set up in her head.

That same evening, Lord Hartleigh made his way to his cousin's lodgings. He had not visited the place in some years, and the closeness and shabbiness of the apartments shocked him, especially in their marked contrast to Basil's elegant attire. Mr Trevelyan was just applying the finishing touches to his ensemble, preparatory to an evening on the town, and he seemed neither surprised nor disconcerted by his cousin's abrupt appearance. "Come in, cuz," he told him coolly. "This is indeed an honour—though not, I must say, unlooked for."

"You expected me?" the earl asked, no whit less coolly.

"Oh, yes, indeed. In fact, I have been on pins and needles the whole day. Even sent my man out for a bottle or two of your favourite. And considering that I had to send ready cash along with him—for neither the vintner nor my valet will advance me another penny—I hope you'll do me the honour to partake of it."

At Lord Hartleigh's nod, he drew out from a small cabinet two glasses. These he minutely inspected, holding them up to the light. He then subjected the wine to the same scrutiny, and, after leisurely satisfying himself on these two counts, served his cousin and himself, and bade the earl be seated. Basil took a chair opposite and launched into a long stream of social chatter in which the weather and Lord Byron's relations with Caro Lamb figured most prominently. The earl bore with him. He knew that his cousin wished to irritate him, and therefore refused to be irritated. Finally, after some twenty minutes of relentless jabber, Basil broke off abruptly: "But then, cuz, I forget that this can't be a social call. I believe you have come on"—he smiled, recalling Isabella's tone that morning a few days ago—"a matter of *business*."

At the earl's nod, he went on, "Then tell me your business—although I believe I can guess it. Do you come on Miss Latham's behalf? I suppose you must, though I confess I'd rather she came as her own emissary."

"I come on her behalf" was the curt reply, "but she has *not* sent me."

"Ah, then perhaps she is still unconscious. How unfortunate that your *ministrations* had so little effect."

Lord Hartleigh suppressed the urge to hurl his glass in

his cousin's face, and, wishing to avoid possible future temptation, he gently put it down. "I believe I'll let that insinuation pass," he answered, his voice just a shade too quiet, "though it does you no credit. For I've known you all your life, Basil, and I do believe you can't help it."

"You needn't patronise me, My Lord—"

The earl went on, as though he hadn't heard, "In fact, it's precisely because you *can't* help yourself that I've come. You seem to have gotten yourself into a surprisingly bad scrape, especially considering the advantages with which you began."

"You don't mean to lecture at me? For if you do, let me warn you that I get a weekly sermon from Aunt Clem. And, uplifting as it may be, it quite adequately meets my needs for that sort of thing."

"I haven't come to lecture. I've come to offer a solution—"

"But, cousin, perhaps I have one already."

"I don't doubt that you do. But it isn't worthy of you, Basil."

Basil's face flushed as he snapped, "Enough of this sanctimony. Let's have the word with no bark on it. In return for something or other, you want me to give the lady up."

"Yes."

"Well, I simply can't imagine what you could offer to compensate. It isn't only that Miss Latham is the perfect solution to all my difficulties. No. I know it'll surprise you—it surprises me—but I've grown rather fond of her. Oh, I'll admit she isn't very pretty; certainly not in my usual style. And she is overly serious and so terribly *responsible*. But I like to hear her laugh, you see. And at close quarters, Edward," he went on in confidential tones, deliberately baiting his cousin, "she is surprisingly appealing. Why, if I were at all poetical, I should write an ode to those delicious lips of hers."

The urge to strangle his cousin nearly overcame Lord Hartleigh, but with superhuman effort he controlled himself, and merely pointed out that in such a case, Basil must, of course, consider Miss Latham's happiness above all things.

"Dear Edward, I should like ever so much to think of nothing but Miss Latham's happiness. Unfortunately, I am forced to consider the feelings of certain other parties."

"And I gather these 'other parties' require certain payments in gold to soothe their tender feelings."

"Why, there you have it, Edward. They are quite tender about their guineas."

"You are telling me you want the money . . . and the girl."

"Yes, of course."

"And you would not consider an offer—say, an annuity which would allow you to pay the more pressing of your debts while still leaving you something to live on." The earl went on to name an amount which nearly took Basil's breath away.

But Mr Trevelyan recovered quickly enough. "Tempting, cousin. But no, it won't do. I mean to have her, Edward. And I recommend you give it up."

The menace in his tone made the earl look up in surprise.

"You mistake me, cousin, if you think to bribe or trick me out of this game. And I believe you know me well enough to understand that I do not speak idly when I warn you away. You have your title. You have your lavish inheritance, which you so casually toss in my face. Be content with those, and find another mama for Lucy. For you will *not* have Isabella Latham."

Now this was odd indeed. Lord Hartleigh had expected a struggle. Basil needed money, and had enough spite to want Isabella just because Edward wanted her. But Edward had hoped that his cousin would eventually be content to escape marriage—as long as he could do so profitably. After all, he had no real hold on Miss Latham. Basil knew Edward wouldn't stand for any more scandal-mongering. So what was it that made the little beast so confident? Another quarter hour's argument made it clear that the little beast

136

had no intention of telling. He just sat there, smiling and smug, unmoved by threats or appeals to his honour or any other of the pleas to which his cousin at length resorted.

"No, Edward," he said, finally. "It won't do. And don't think to try to steal her away, for you may force some matters which can only cause my darling—and her family—tremendous pain."

And that was as much as could be gotten out of him. Edward took his leave calmly enough, but inwardly he seethed with rage and frustration. For without knowing what new villainy his cousin was contemplating, he hardly dared press Isabella to abandon the wretch.

Yet Lord Hartleigh knew he could not keep away from her—not if his life depended upon it. It was all he could do to stay away until tomorrow; all he could do to keep from rushing to her house and carrying her away—now—in the middle of the night.

Basil, meanwhile, was not quite as sanguine as he had appeared to his cousin. Before him on the table, next to a half-empty wineglass, was a much-creased letter.

It had taken a great deal of investigating, not to mention associating with persons Basil preferred not to know, before he had discovered Captain Macomber. Recently arrived from India, and an old friend of Captain Williams (now better known as Viscount Deverell), the lonely widower had been pleased to make the acquaintance of Mademoiselle Celestine. And Celestine, of course, required payment for entertaining the Captain. For after all, she had not only discovered his mission but—unlooked-for prize—had relieved the retired seaman of the precious scrap of paper.

> . . . to learn the truth after all these years—or at least, some part of the truth. I do not know what words he used to convince Maria, but if they were at all like those he wrote to me, the man must have had the very Devil at his ear, prompting him.
> And yet you must think it was my own damned fault, do you not? That I made no effort, when

opportunity finally came, to see Maria myself—or to enquire more closely into the circumstances of their marriage and the birth of the child. But I thought to spare her trouble. And in truth, my pride was hurt that she had not waited longer before remarrying.

I know this is sorry repayment for all you have done for me these many years—yet I pray you understand the circumstances which prevented my revealing myself even to you, my closest friend. And I hope you will find it in your great and generous heart to forgive me.

Though he would not admit it, the heartache of Deverell's letter moved him. Mired as he was in his debts and machinations, Basil wished, for a moment, that he had accepted Edward's offer. But no. Just to keep out of prison would take up the whole of the annuity. With nothing over to live on, there would be further debts. No, it wouldn't do. And after all he'd done and risked, he was not about to leave to Edward the promised pleasures of that delicious mouth, that slim and sensuous body . . . and that low, intoxicating laughter.

16

Mama certainly was energetic today, Isabella thought, as she sat with her book in the now-restored small parlour. Maria had begun by convincing Aunt Charlotte to visit with Lady Bertram. "She begs for word of Isabella," Maria had sighed, "and will not be content with my note." In response to Lady Belcomb's protests that the countess could come see for herself, Maria provided seven or eight contradictory reasons why she could not, finally adding that she believed one of those Stirewells—or all of them—were expected, and Lady Bertram could not stir from home. This last silenced Charlotte, who immediately called for her daughter, found fault with her dress, made her change twice, and at length left the house, dragging the confused Veronica behind her.

Alicia was dispatched with her maid on a shopping expedition, and several dozen servants were provided with suitable occupations to keep them at some distance from the room in which Isabella sat reading. Mrs Latham then had a confidential interview with the butler, who had very little trouble memorising the names of those whose visits would not be too fatiguing for her daughter.

And so, when Lord Hartleigh called, he found only Isabella and her mother at home. He had no sooner entered the room and presented Isabella with a bouquet (which she promptly dropped, in her agitation) than the indefatigable Maria suddenly recalled an urgent matter for the kitchen, and was gone before her daughter had time to object.

But Mama's treachery was forgotten in an instant, for the earl immediately lowered himself onto the sofa next to his darling, took her hand, and pressed it to his lips. This proving insufficient expression of his feelings, he took her in his arms and kissed her until she was dizzy.

Now *he* knew it wasn't right, and *she* knew it wasn't right, but several blissful minutes passed before either of them was remotely inclined to act upon what they knew. As it was, Isabella was the first to act, but she made such a poor attempt at indignation that Lord Hartleigh immediately forgot the abject apology he owed her and told her instead that he'd been frightened half to death on her account, that his life was not worth living without her, that he needed her, wanted her, and other such romantical nonsense, which he then summarised by telling her that he loved her. And when those intelligent blue eyes looked back so adoringly into his, he silently bade the proprieties—and his cousin—to the Devil, and kissed her again.

Now this was all so very pleasant that it quickly began to grow indecent, for Lord Hartleigh was not *quite* content to plant tender kisses on Isabella's lips. He remembered a trail he had blazed a few nights ago, and let his lips travel upon it once again—from the ticklish spot behind her ear down along her neck to her shoulders to the not-insurmountable barrier of her bodice. And Isabella, to her shame, had tangled his lordship's hair into disorderly curls and had even disarranged the perfect folds of his cravat; not, as one would expect, in the struggle to protect her virtue, but rather to bring it into immediate danger.

However, as his lordship's gentle hands began exploring new territories, the danger finally penetrated Isabella's brain, and in the midst of a startlingly warm and enthusiastic response, she suddenly remembered that she was supposed to be engaged to someone else altogether. "Oh, no. Stop," she gasped. "Please stop."

Now it is very true that Lord Hartleigh had "unusually high notions of duty" and a powerful sense of honor and right. But at the moment, having already sent Propriety to the Devil, he was exceedingly loath to recall it. He was, moreover, extremely reluctant to leave off his highly satisfactory explorations of Isabella's person. For though he did truly esteem and admire Miss Latham, and had great respect for her intellect, he was driven, at the moment, by naked lust. Every taste and touch was so delicious that he thought only of having more, and had completely forgotten everything else.

But now, for some unaccountable reason, she was telling him to stop. He pretended not to hear, and when her pleas grew more urgent, he tried to stop them with kisses. But she now refused to cooperate and was pushing him away. "Please stop," she hissed. "Mama will be back any minute."

Mama? Heated and breathless, he drew back and looked at her. Her silky hair had come loose from its pins, and one strand tickled the corner of her mouth. Lovingly, he brushed it aside, letting his fingers linger on her soft cheek, which grew bright pink under his gaze. "I quite forgot your mother," he said softly. "I thought—I wished—we were just . . . we two."

Feeling herself melting again, Isabella moved a few inches away from him, and strove—rather ineffectually, for her hands were trembling—to restore herself to rights. "For some reason," she muttered, trying to gather together some shreds of dignity, "I seem to forget myself in your company, My Lord. However, I hope you will remember that I've recently had a concussion, and cannot be held completely accountable for my actions."

Despite his frustration—for Lord Hartleigh did truly feel like a starving man who'd been invited to inhale the fragrance of a great feast and then forbidden to partake of it—despite this agony, his lips twitched with suppressed laughter as he gravely replied, "I'm fully aware of that, Miss Latham, and can only offer you my abject apologies for taking advantage of your . . . your weakened condition."

"Yes," she agreed, rather absently. Then, noting that he was as dishevelled as herself, she added, "Perhaps you should repair your cravat, sir."

Solemnly, he assured her that this was impossible. "A cravat," he whispered wickedly, "is very much like a reputation, Miss Latham. Once damaged, it cannot be repaired." Ignoring her gasp, he went on: "Except perhaps by some other, higher power. My valet can easily replace the neckcloth, you see. But your reputation is a matter for the parson. You will have to marry me as soon as possible." He reached for her, but she quickly got up from the sofa and crossed to the other side of the room. "I can't," she said.

"You've made some foolish promise to Basil—or, rather, he's tricked you into a foolish promise. Come, Isabella, you can't seriously believe you're obliged to him in any way—"

"I am. I gave my word."

"If you discover that a man has cheated at cards, you do not proceed to pay him the money he's cheated from you." Impatient, he rose and strode across the room. Grasping her shoulders, he said softly, "Look at me and tell me you don't care for me. Tell me that you love him instead and want to be his wife. Tell me that and I'll go away and never trouble you again."

She hesitated, then met his eyes and smiled. "You know I can tell you no such thing."

"Good," he replied, then added with a wicked smile that made her heart flutter, "Then I propose we continue where we left off some moments ago, so that your mother will find us in a suitably compromising position. I don't plan to allow you the opportunity to change your mind later—when I've gone, and your infernal conscience tweaks you." So saying, he lifted her in his arms and carried her back to the sofa. He was just commencing yet another loving assault on her person when there was a rustling at the door.

"Now isn't that a pretty picture," Basil drawled as he sauntered into the room.

Isabella bolted upright, nearly knocking the earl off the sofa in the process. "We could ignore him," Lord Hartleigh muttered, disentangling himself from her gown. "Perhaps he'd go away."

"Certainly not," said Basil. He dropped his elegant form into a chair opposite, then pulled out his glass and calmly surveyed the scene before him. "Good heavens, Edward, your cravat is a disgrace. I suspected my fiancée had a passionate nature, but I did not think she had no respect for a man's neckcloth."

She is *not* your fiancée," Edward growled.

"Oh, but she is. Hasn't she thought to tell you, cuz? Carried away by the heat of the moment, no doubt. But really, Isabella, you might have at least waited until *after* we were wed. I declare, you haven't the faintest notion how to go on in Society, do you, my love? First you get married, *then* you're unfaithful. Not the other way around. It just isn't done."

"Isabella has always had an odd way of doing things, Mr Trevelyan. She has had an unusual upbringing, you see. All those ledgers. . . ." This last trailed off into a sigh, as Maria Latham stepped into the room. Her weary gaze drifted from one to the next to the next, and she sighed again. "I do hope Fredericks does not subject us to any more visitors today. I find dramatic entrances most fatiguing." Acknowledging the gentlemen's bows, she wandered toward the sofa and, having waved Lord Hartleigh to another chair, took her place beside her daughter. "Isabella," she said, "I think you have been naughty."

"She has had a concussion," the earl began, but a speaking look from Mrs Latham quelled him.

"A concussion is no excuse for bad manners. Pray apologise to Mr Trevelyan, Isabella—"

"Mama!" Isabella gasped.

"And tell him to go away. Under the circumstances, he cannot wish to marry you."

"Oh, but I do, Mrs Latham. I am a very forgiving sort of person."

"Are you indeed?" The blue-green eyes met his, and Basil reddened slightly, but he went on nonetheless. "Yes, quite forgiving. She has had a concussion and my wicked cousin has attempted to take advantage of her weakened condition—"

"He did not!" Isabella cried, irritated at being treated like somebody's senile aunt.

"Well then, my love, I forgive you anyhow. I'm sure you had a good reason," Basil replied, with a maddeningly patronising smile.

"Yes, I did," she snapped. "I love him—and I'm going to marry him—aren't I?" She faltered, looking at Lord Hartleigh.

"Of course you are," that gentleman reassured her.

"There you are, Mr Trevelyan," said Mrs Latham, in tones of exhausted yet patient forbearance. "She means to marry your cousin. And now you may go away."

"Well, she's not going to marry him for all she thinks so at the moment." The topaz eyes glittered under half-closed lids as Basil toyed with his cane. "For one thing, what will her father say?"

There was silence in the room. Two faces stared at him as though he had suddenly gone mad. But there was a tiny crease between Maria Latham's brows as she watched him, warily. Isabella was the first to speak. "What are you saying, Basil? Papa died five years ago."

"Matthew Latham died five years ago. Your papa is alive and well. If he is not already in London, he is on his way—from India."

The tale had been told, and Isabella sat in stunned silence as her two suitors were summarily dismissed. Viscount Deverell—her father—and Mama had never said a word; not all these years, no, and not even today, as Basil's strangely harsh voice had gone on and on.

Yes, Harry Deverell had gone to sea. And yes, when Maria had run away, it was long after he'd left home. But that had been part of the plan—so that none would connect Maria's disappearance with Harry. And according to plans made well in advance, the two had married in an obscure town on the Cornish coast. The young couple had a few months of bliss before Harry was called away. He had just left when Maria discovered she was pregnant. And then, in less than a week, there was the accident, and Harry was presumed drowned.

What came next brought an aching lump to Isabella's throat, but she couldn't cry. What would she have done in her mother's place? Would she have waited, hoping against hope that it was all a terrible mistake? Would her pride have allowed her to present herself to her unsuspecting in-laws and demand that they care for her and the unborn child she claimed was Harry's?

Maria reentered the room, but she did not approach her daughter. Instead, she stood by the window, gazing out in her usual abstracted manner. It was only now that Isabella associated that look with the sailor's wife, gazing out to sea. As though she'd read her daughter's thoughts, Maria said, softly, "I did not know which way to turn. I had my marriage lines, but even so, it was more than likely we'd forfeited any claims to our families' support by going against their wishes. And even if they had determined it was their duty to help—they had little enough for themselves. When Matt Latham offered to marry me, it seemed the only solution. Harry was dead. I believed neither my nor Harry's family would take me in. And I had more than myself to consider. I did not want Harry's child to grow up in misery and want." Her voice never changed, never trembled. It was steady and detached throughout her recitation; and it did sound curiously like a recitation of a piece of fiction, rather than the true story of the ordeal she'd undergone.

Isabella got up and moved across the room to join her mother at the window. "In your place, Mama, I think I would have done the same. But why did you never tell me?"

"Neither when I thought Harry dead nor in recent months, when I knew him to be alive, did I feel it necessary to burden you with our secret."

"But surely when you learned—"

"No. I knew nothing of his life for all those years. I knew nothing of his wishes in the matter. I had rather even Mr Trevelyan be the first to tell you than that I do so without Harry's expressed consent."

Isabella took her mother's hand. "Poor Mama," she murmured.

"No," said Maria. "You must not pity me. Matt Latham did a terrible thing in driving your papa away. But he did love me. And except for betraying Harry, who had been his friend—Matt had even helped us plan our elopement, you know—well, apart from that, and those disastrous financial undertakings, Matthew Latham was a tolerable husband." The bored tone had crept back into her voice—and oddly enough, Isabella was relieved to hear it.

"But he knew my . . . my father was alive—and he never told you."

"Your father regained his memory almost a year later; he'd been struck in the head during some scuffle or other." Maria smiled, remembering Harry Deverell's quick temper. "He wrote to Matthew Latham—not his parents or brothers—first, asking him to break the news gently to me. But instead, my new husband wrote back, telling of the marriage, lying about the date of your birth, and, apparently, giving your father to understand that to reclaim me as his bride was to ruin me. I knew nothing of this. Nor did your uncle know of it, until a very short time ago. I had written to him that I suspected Mr Trevelyan knew something of the story. And Henry had that same day received a letter from a Captain Macomber, a friend of your father's, who related as much of the story as your father had finally confided to him. Apparently, once Harry received Matt's letter, he had determined to leave the past in darkness forever, and never to return to England. It was only the death of his older brothers that persuaded him otherwise. And in the course of corresponding with his family, he learned a bit more about us, and soon realized that Matthew Latham had lied about your birth."

Maria gently led her daughter away from the window, back to the sofa. Gazing earnestly at her, she went on, "Isabella, perhaps now you'll understand my reluctance to abandon you to the tender mercies of Mr Trevelyan. Matt Latham did a terrible thing, but he did it because he loved me. And because he loved me, I was able to have a tolerable life, though I was only moderately fond of him. I do not say that you may not have some mild affection for Mr Trevelyan. It is not difficult to see that there is a decent sort of heart there, somewhere underneath his poses and machinations. But he cannot truly love you. How could he, and wave the family's dirty linen in your face? To marry him would be to march merrily off to your own perdition."

"But he has threatened to spread your story—"

"Good heavens, Isabella. Caro Lamb stalks Byron everywhere he goes and he makes sport of her to his friends. I'm sorry to disillusion you, but their antics will quite take the shine out of this Gothic ancient history of ours. And as to a little accidental bigamy that happened more than a quarter century ago—why, has not our Regent made bigamy quite fashionable? No, Society will buzz about us for a day or two, and then Caro will commit another outrageous act, and they will quite forget all about us. And you seem to forget—as Mr Trevelyan has—that at some point he will have to answer to Harry Deverell, if he does not first have to answer to Lord Hartleigh. No, my love. I do not think we need trouble ourselves overmuch with your nefarious so-called fiancé."

17

"There," said the lovely Celestine as she sealed the note and handed it to her visitor. "That'll fetch him. But I want you to know I'd never play him such a sorry trick if I wasn't about to get the toss myself, and need the money so badly."

"He won't suffer long for it," Henry Latham assured her. "Not if he's sensible."

"Ah, but he isn't," the young woman sighed. "Or he wouldn't be in such a fix, now would he?"

The middle-aged gentleman merely shrugged, and with a courtly bow of which she somehow wished she were worthy, he handed her a bulky envelope and left.

"You think," the earl snarled, as the two cousins made their ignominious exit from the house, "that because you are my cousin, I shall not call you out. Well, you are sadly mistaken—"

"I had rather thought to call *you* out," Basil retorted, "considering that she is *my* betrothed. If anyone has been insulted, it is I."

"Why, you wretched little slug!" the earl cried, grasping his cousin by the throat.

"My neckcloth, Edward. You're forgetting yourself." This last came out in a gasp, for the Earl of Hartleigh was, in fact, to the considerable interest of several passers-by, attempting to throttle his cousin. Words having no effect, Basil gave his lordship a sharp kick in the shin. The sudden pain made the earl loosen his grip, so that Basil was able to wrench his cousin's fingers from his neck. "Now," he croaked, "you are making a spectacle of yourself, and unless you desire to cause a riot on your darling's doorstep, I advise you to mind your manners."

Thus recalled to his surroundings, the still-furious Lord Hartleigh stepped away. "You have the effrontery to babble of manners. How dare you subject that girl to that villainous tale?"

"I did not make it up" was the tart rejoinder. But Basil's ears reddened—evidence that it was not only attempted strangulation which worked on him at present.

"True or not, it was infamous to tell it. It was obvious from the start that the poor girl had no idea—"

"That is her mother's fault." Basil attempted to adjust his neckcloth, but quickly gave it up and turned to face his cousin. "If you truly do wish to protect your precious Isabella, I advise you to keep your hands to yourself—not only in my case, but in hers as well. Good day, cousin." And he quickly took himself away.

For a moment, the earl debated whether to pursue him, but reason prevailed, and he took himself in the opposite direction, trying to collect his disordered thoughts.

Ever since the day when Lucy had been misplaced, it seemed that the Earl of Hartleigh was doomed to travel the streets of London in one state of fit or another. He did not understand why he, as well as his cousin, had been so cavalierly dismissed by Mrs Latham. Yes, Isabella needed comforting, but who better than himself to minister to her needs? And he had not been given opportunity to assure her that no matter what Basil knew or threatened to tell, she would be Countess of Hartleigh, and scandal would not be allowed to touch her.

Oh, scandal there would be, no doubt. But it was ancient history, and would soon be washed away as a new tide of gossip swept in. Why, by the time Harry Deverell made his way to London, it would all be forgotten . . . wouldn't it? But if it were not forgotten, could he truly protect her from the pain? And if he could not, could he bear to watch it, and know he was the cause of it? For Basil had been adamant: The betrothal would be honoured, or he'd go directly to Sally Jersey with the whole sorry tale. That Basil should have sunk so low. . . . He hadn't used to be cruel—only selfish and irresponsible.

As he walked slowly in the direction of his aunt's house, Lord Hartleigh contemplated the twisted tale he had just heard. What had Matt written to Harry Deverell to drive him away, to discourage him so completely from attempting to see Maria himself, to drive him from England forever? Some appeal to Harry's honour, no doubt. And if Harry had loved Maria enough to run off with her secretly, to risk being cut off forever from his family, then he would be unable to bear living on the same island, knowing she belonged to another. At least, if Lord Hartleigh compared it to his own state of mind, then this must be the case. No, as Harry had reasoned it, he could not come back to life. He could not reclaim his wife. And should any discover the early marriage, his being alive would make her guilty of bigamy. Gossip would not take into account the circumstances. Her youth and her naïveté would be held against her, particularly by the spiteful old cats who resented her beauty. For she had been a beauty; was still.

And now Isabella? Even if she escaped relatively unscathed from the scandal, her Latham cousins' prospects would be ruined. And though their mother might be a social climber, the daughters—or Alicia, at least—seemed well-bred enough to move into a higher social strata.

But with no blood claim on Isabella, their fragile hold on Society would be cut away. Alicia would be forced to retire to Westford; no, she would not. The Countess of Hartleigh could take under her wing whomever she chose, and all but the very highest sticklers would be happy to recognize her protégées.

No, Isabella would not suffer her mother's fate. She would not be forced to sacrifice her future happiness on the simple threat of scandal. Basil was a fool, a desperate fool, and he would not have his way.

Abruptly, Lord Hartleigh turned and made his way back to Lord Belcomb's residence.

"Lord Hartleigh, you do tax my patience," said Mrs Latham as he was shown into the room. "Did I not just half an hour ago tell you and your cousin to go away until further notice?"

The earl maintained that he would *not* go away, that he intended to marry Isabella, and that he intended to do so immediately.

"Gracious God!" Isabella cried. "Are you mad? Didn't you hear what Basil said?"

"Yes. And that's why time is of the essence. I'm going now to procure a special licence. While I'm gone, your maid can help you pack."

"Pack?" she echoed blankly. "What are you saying?" She turned to her mother. "What is he saying?"

Maria Latham dropped gracefully onto the sofa. "You are excessively slow today, Isabella. It must be the concussion. Lord Hartleigh wishes to carry you off somewhere to be married. Under the circumstances, it would be best to begin packing immediately. I expect you'll be going some distance?" She lifted an enquiring gaze to Lord Hartleigh.

"To Hartleigh Hall. We'll stop for Aunt Clem, first, of course," he added. "Unless you wish to chaperone us, madam?"

"No, thank you. I find all this display of energy excessively fatiguing. And someone must remain to explain the situation to dear Charlotte. She'll be dreadfully cross." A low chuckle expressed the degree of concern Maria felt for her sister-in-law's delicate sensibilities.

"Then please make haste, my love," said Lord Hartleigh. He dropped a gentle kiss on Isabella's forehead, bowed to Mrs. Latham, and was gone, leaving his intended bride to gaze wonderingly after him.

"I still cannot decide whether he or his cousin is more handsome, but on the whole, I think he will make a better husband. Well, Isabella? Are you going to stand there gaping all day?"

"But, Mama, Basil just said—"

"Yes, and if you don't make haste, you will not have the pleasant opportunity of thwarting Mr Trevelyan. Why, what scandal do you think he'll dare provoke once you are married?"

"But, Mama—"

"Isabella, you're exhausting me. Please go away and pack."

Although he'd taken a calm leave of his cousin, Mr Trevelyan was an exceedingly uncomfortable man at the moment. He cringed at the greetings of acquaintances as he strode down the street, and may have been perceived to slink into the privacy of his club. But there was no privacy for him, really, for he must bear *himself* company, and that self had, in the last hour, turned into a decidedly unpleasant fellow—one whom, in fact, he'd prefer not to know.

First, of course, there was the shock and the blow to his vanity of coming upon Miss Latham in the embrace of his cousin. That she returned the embrace enthusiastically was obvious, even to an imbecile. And Basil greatly feared that this was exactly what he had become. He politely declined the various invitations to join his cronies, and found instead a quiet corner, where he sulked behind a newspaper. Hating himself, he was yet most angry with Isabella, for it was she who had reduced him to this state—reduced him to the level of a slug, as his cousin had so aptly labelled him.

Perhaps he was unfair to Isabella in this; yet it must be known that for all his sophistication, Basil lacked a certain important experience: He had never in his thirty years been rejected in favour of another by a female.

True, his aim had not been high. Married ladies and members of the *demimonde* had always been his targets.

And those young virgins with whom he had occasionally flirted had all been so naïve—and astoundingly stupid—that he had never been tempted to more than flirtation. In fact, it was Isabella's intelligence which was her undoing, for she didn't immediately bore him. Had she done, he might have more easily torn himself away. No, the matter was that from his doting mother to the complaisant matrons and eager Cyprians, women had always been captivated by him. And thus, never having experienced rejection, he had no philosophy to guide him. He had no idea how to shrug it off.

Perhaps he'd known in his heart that, in the end, Isabella would not have him. Perhaps he'd known even before that morning when she'd so stiffly outlined her "conditions" and promised herself to him—then winced at his kiss. Certainly he'd known it this afternoon, when he'd made his unwelcome entrance.

But the knowing was of no use to him, since it didn't show him how to salvage his wounded vanity. And of course, added to wounded vanity was the harsh reality of an army of creditors, lying in wait.

It was not surprising, then, that he'd revealed what he knew of Maria Latham's history; nor was it surprising that he'd stooped to blackmail. But he found it strange, and definitely unpleasant, to realise the whole while (indeed, even as the first words were out of his mouth) that in doing so, he had abandoned the ranks of civilised human beings and sunk to the level of vermin.

And now what would he do? Common sense told him to give it up as a bad job and make immediate arrangements for a flight to the Continent. Freddie would loan him the money. Good God, even Edward would help him, would do anything to see the back of him. And then there were friends he could join, for Napoleon had not the entire continent in his grasp, after all. But what would he live on?

One moment Basil was determined on flight; he would live somehow. The next, flight was impossible. And so he went, back and forth, until Celestine's note arrived, and then he thought he need not make so critical a decision at this very minute. First, he would see what the beautiful lady wanted.

No, Mr Trevelyan was not at his lodgings. No, the servant at the club told him, Mr Trevelyan had left hours before. No, none of the club members knew where he'd gone. But Sir Eliot gave a knowing wink as he remarked that he believed Basil had had an urgent message from one of his ladybirds.

Lord Tuttlehope blushed as he knocked on the door. The little French maid's seductive smile only compounded his embarrassment as he stammeringly asked for Mademoiselle Celestine. The maid was so sorry, but mam'selle was engaged with a visitor. He was about to leave then, but screwed up his courage even as the door was closing in his face. "It's demmed urgent," he whispered hoarsely. "A message. Would you be kind enough—"

"But of course," the girl simpered.

"Then please tell Mr Trevelyan—"

"Oh, no, monsieur. Mr Trevelyan is not here." Perhaps monsieur was afflicted with a facial tick, for he blinked so. "It is another gentleman," she explained in a conspiratorial whisper.

Well, he had done his best. And to tell the truth, Freddie breathed a sigh of relief as he reached the street. For had he found Basil and told him what was in the wind, it was certain that his darling Alicia would never speak to him again.

18

It was nearly dawn when Basil opened his eyes. Only a faint grey light filtered through the drapes, but to him it was a blinding explosion which set off a sympathetic thundering in his brain. The wench must have drugged him, he thought, but had no time to consider more before blessed unconsciousness overtook him once again.

When he reawakened, the light was much stronger, but the thundering in his head had subsided to a dull throbbing, and he was able to look about him. It was not Celestine's bedroom; that much was certain. And it was not his own. He wasn't sure, but he thought he detected the faint smell of sea air. Perhaps that was what made his stomach rumble so. Where, then, was he?

As though in answer to his silent question, a plumpish, middle-aged gent who put Basil immediately in mind of a muffin, came to the doorway.

"Ah, you are awake, Mr Trevelyan," said the muffin in the kindliest of tones. "Then let us see what we can do about finding you some nourishment."

"Who the devil are you?" Basil snapped, as he hauled himself up, painfully, to a sitting position. But the gent had disappeared as quickly and silently as he had come, and Mr Trevelyan was left to simmer for a quarter hour before he reappeared. By that time, Basil had managed to crawl out of the bed and make some poor effort at dressing himself—a task rendered extraordinarily difficult by his trembling hands and weak, throbbing head. "Who the devil are you?" he repeated as the stranger placed a breakfast tray on the small table which stood in the darkest corner of the room.

"Latham," said the gent. "Henry Latham, at your service. And I do hope you'll consent to eat something, sir, for you look a bit peakish this morning."

The topaz eyes narrowed, although the effort cost some pain, as Basil asked hoarsely, "How do I know you haven't drugged that too?"

"Why, Mr Trevelyan, what would be the purpose in that?" Mr Latham replied mildly.

"It would be of a piece with the rest of it, wouldn't it?" But hunger gnawed at the young man. How long was it since he'd last eaten? How much time had passed since Celestine had put that glass of wine in his hand? He remembered—or maybe he'd only dreamed it—being jolted in a coach. And an inn. And more wine. And Celestine—or another woman. And apparently they were all in league with this kindly old muffin, who continued to smile innocently at him. The aroma of eggs, ham, toast, and coffee beckoned, however, and Basil determined to postpone further enquiries until he had recovered his strength.

But even as he fell to his meal, he wondered at it—at his sitting there eating a breakfast while Isabella's uncle sat benevolently watching him. It must be a dream, still. At length, as Basil was sipping his second cup of coffee, Henry Latham quietly remarked that he owed the young man an explanation.

"Ah," Basil murmured. "A dream with an explanation. So you mean to tell me you are not a figment of my overactive imagination?"

"No, Mr Trevelyan. But I would hope to play a beneficial role in your life."

Basil quirked an eyebrow. "You mean to *help* me?" At the other's nod, he went on, "Then you have a devilish odd way of going about it, my good man. I do not usually have to be drugged into accepting aid."

"Well, you see, sir, I was concerned that you'd create difficulties."

"I *never* stand in the way of charitable efforts on my behalf—"

"And I had to be sure," Henry continued, "that my niece was safely out of danger before I put my proposal to you."

The coffee cup clattered to its saucer. "The devil you did," Basil sputtered. "Where is she?"

"With your cousin, sir. Or I should say," he corrected with a gentle smile, "with her husband."

"That scheming—you conniving thief!" Basil shrieked, jumping up. "I'll have the law on you. Assault. Kidnapping." He went on with a list of various criminal complaints, punctuated at intervals with curses on his perfidious fiancée and cousin and their families, all of which Henry Latham bore patiently—benignly, in fact—as though it were an outpouring of good wishes.

"Yes," he responded, as Basil paused to catch his breath, "I can see how very disappointing it is for you, Mr Trevelyan. But you must see that Isabella's happiness must come first with all of us."

"Happiness," Basil snarled. "We'll see how much joy she has of her marriage. And the rest of your wretched, conniving family. What kind of a life do you think she'll have when all of London learns of her mother's hasty, bigamous marriage—and of your brother's part in Harry Deverell's disappearance?"

"Why, as to that," said Henry, calmly, "there's no telling how the wind will blow. Mayhap they'll make out Maria as the victim of my unscrupulous brother. And if so, 'tis only my family that must bear the shame. Alicia will simply have to come home with me and make the best of her prospects among her own kind."

"And give up her baron?" Basil sneered.

"She's no business with such. A plain 'Mrs' is all the title she needs."

"You think to convince me that the scandal doesn't matter?"

"No, Mr Trevelyan. For the plain fact is, much as I think my daughter was encouraged to look too high above herself—well, we'd all rather keep the shameful story quiet. And that is why I appeal to your better nature. Isabella has married your cousin. What's done is done."

"No, Mr Latham. It is not done. You've stolen my last chance from me, and I will not go down to destruction without some revenge. And if it is only the satisfaction of bringing misery and shame down on your whole miserable family, then I will have it." But even as he spoke, Basil knew he was defeated. What good would it do him? Driving Alicia from society would not pay his debts—and it *would* alienate Freddie. Dragging Isabella's family through the mire of scandal would not keep him from debtors' prison. The amber cat eyes were bleak with despair. Debtors' prison.

But as his gaze fell upon the open, kindly countenance before him, he realised that he had lost more than a fortune. Somewhere in the place where his heart was supposed to be had been a faint, unacknowledged hope: that Isabella would somehow make things right for him. Perhaps he'd even imagined she'd one day come to love him, and thereby prove that he'd done no wrong; had acted in her best interests, in fact. But he'd deluded himself. It was only now, as he contemplated his dismal future, as he thought of the friends who'd fall away when the prison walls closed around him, that he realised how completely alone he was. And if any suspected the level to which he had sunk . . . well, who *would* come to his aid?

But Henry Latham was speaking, and Basil forced himself to attend.

"You see, Mr Trevelyan," he was saying, "I do feel responsible, in a way. For I saw what you were about some time ago, when my sister-in-law wrote to me. You may not believe it, but none of us—excepting Matt—knew the whole truth of the story. I learned of it myself the very day I'd heard from Maria. I was shocked then, but hesitated to act until I knew more—about *you,* especially. Maybe I should have been more forthright. Maybe I should have spoken with you directly, man to man, and we could have come to some agreeable arrangement."

Basil gave a morose growl in reply.

"At any rate, I have a proposition for you." He went on to explain that he had bought up more than half of Basil's notes—"for there has not been time to locate all your creditors. It really is astonishing," Henry mumbled, half to himself, "the amount of credit a man in your position is extended; no wonder so many of you are ruined so young. But at any rate," he went on, more brightly, "I believe something can be done."

"What the devil are you talking about? Bought up my notes? Why, there must be—"

Henry put up his hand. "Outrageous is what it is. Why, the interest alone could keep a family of six comfortably for several years. Well, what's done is done."

"I am undone, is what it is. You are saying that if I don't consent to curb my tongue, you'll call in my markers and have me clapped into prison."

"Why, that's the long and short of it. But it doesn't solve your problems, now does it, Mr Trevelyan? For how are you to get *out* of prison again?"

"I appreciate your concern, sir, but as I have no means of escaping to the Continent, and as prison most certainly won't agree with me, you can look forward to my early demise." Basil flung himself into a chair to contemplate this untimely end.

"Do you think India might be more agreeable?"

"India," Basil repeated dully.

"For I have some business there and could use a clever fellow."

"Business. In India." Basil looked up from his mournful meditations to meet the kindly brown eyes. "You are proposing I go into *trade?*" He said it as though he'd been asked to consider contracting a loathsome disease.

But Mr Latham explained that the young man would not be expected to dirty his hands with trade. Only to keep a lookout on things, to hobnob a bit with the local higher-ups. "It could be very profitable, sir, for both of us. A few choice pieces of information at the right time would pay handsomely. You might even be put in the way of information which would be of use to His Majesty's government."

Basil's eyes flew open at this

"For to be quite frank with you, sir, I am rather in such a way myself. Business is inextricably tied to politics, you know. And even such as I have some concern in keeping our enemies at bay."

"You suggest that I take up the sort of endeavour my cousin was forced to give up?"

"In the way of business, no more. And as to business, why, I'd guess that with your talents, you'd earn enough to cover all your debts in two or three years—and come away with something handsome in the bargain. Are you game, sir?"

Basil thought quickly. He could try to convince Aunt Clem to hold off the creditors. But would she? And for how long? And if she would not or could not, he must leave England . . . with nothing to live on. No, there was nothing to be decided. It meant work; the very idea made his blood run cold. But it could mean adventure, of sorts. And maybe a bit of glory might drift his way and cling to him. A hero. He might even be a hero. In less than two minutes, in a very bored, very resigned voice, he replied, "Well, it seems I have no choice. Yes, Mr Latham, I am—as you say—game."

"Alone at last," murmured the earl, closing the bedroom door behind him. "No mama, no aunts, no cousins, no blasted servants—come to think of it, there *are* the servants, and with my luck . . . perhaps I'd better bar the door?"

"In your own home, My Lord?" Though her voice was

playful, Isabella was suddenly nervous. For here she was, alone with her new husband in his—their—bedroom, and no officious relatives likely to burst in to protect her virtue. Good heavens. She was married to him and was not *supposed* to protect her virtue. Quite the opposite, in fact. She blushed and, seeing the dark eyes gazing at her with such intensity, backed away . . . and stumbled against the bedpost.

"Better safe than sorry," Lord Hartleigh muttered as he turned the key in the lock. A few quick strides and he was across the room, but to his amazement, his bride retreated. "Is something wrong, my love?" Then, noting the blush that spread from her cheeks to her throat, his lip quivered, and he whispered, "Surely you're not afraid of me, Isabella."

"No. Yes" was the subdued reply.

"Darling, you don't think I'm going to murder you."

"No."

"And after all, you've had some sample . . . or at least a prologue."

A faint smile began to curve her lips.

He held out his arms. "Then come to me . . . and let us complete what was so rudely interrupted a few days ago. As I recall, you have a most winning way with a neckcloth."

Taking a deep breath to slow her pounding heart, Isabella walked into his open arms and laid her head on his chest. She could hear his heart pounding, too. But then his arms closed around her, pulling her close. She felt his warm breath at her ear, and had only a moment to mutter something about a concussion before his lips were pressing softly on hers. Then love took over (and lust, too, it must be admitted), and the earl's cravat went bravely to its destruction.

Maria raised her world-weary eyes from her book. "Who?" she enquired of Lord Hartleigh's discomfitted butler.

Life in her brother's household had become increasingly uncomfortable after Isabella's departure. Although Charlotte had come rather quickly to accept Veronica's preference for the Stirewell heir, she could not forgive Maria the Earl of Hartleigh's defection. If Isabella and Maria had not conspired to entrap him, he would never have been enticed away from Veronica. That Lord Hartleigh had never evidenced the remotest interest in Veronica was all put down to the conspiracy. And then, of course, there was Lord Tuttlehope, who, out of the clear blue sky, up and offered for Alicia Latham. If that wasn't conspiracy, Lady Belcomb didn't know what it was—and she would not be surprised to learn that Napoleon was at the bottom of it.

It was the conspiracy theory that finally wore out Maria's patience. And despite her brother's pleadings, she accepted the Earl and Countess of Hartleigh's invitation to live with them.

Now it may be counted odd in a newly wed couple to invite a parent to come live with them. And certainly Isabella had wondered at her husband's proposing it, even before they learned how difficult life had become for Maria in London. But when questioned, the earl calmly replied that Maria was not the interfering sort, and that it was more than likely they would be unaware most of the time that she was even about.

In truth, the house and grounds of the Hartleigh estate were so vast that Maria could be lost for weeks before anyone noticed. And as it turned out, only Burgess, the earl's terrifying butler, who for thirty years had ruled his household with a rod of iron, was at all disturbed by the new resident. For from the first, when Maria had looked up at his immense height and stern demeanor with that faint indulgent smile—a smile one would give a great overgrown puppy, or a very small boy, as one patted him fondly on the head—the butler had been frightened of her. He lived in terror that one day this slender, lackadaisical, unpredictable woman *would* pat him on his head, and all his authority would crumble into dust. But for all that, he was fond of the lady, and very sharp with any staff member who so much as hinted a question of Mrs Latham's mental faculties.

Still, she was at it again. He had announced the visitor, and she acted as though he were saying it only to tease her. As she looked up at him, Burgess had the unaccountable sensation that he had done something *naughty*.

Nonetheless, his face was emotionless as he repeated, patiently, "Lord Deverell, madam. I have explained that you are not at home today, but—"

"Confound it, Maria, I've been up and down the whole blasted island looking for you, and this fellow has the effrontery to tell me you're not at home." A tall, fair-haired, quite handsome gentleman in his late forties pushed past the protective butler.

"Why, Harry," said Maria.

"Don't 'Harry' me, you unfaithful female. Where's Isabella?"

"Well, I'm sure I don't know," the female replied, sinking gracefully back onto her cushions. "Somewhere about. Perhaps Burgess can tell you."

"The Countess of Hartleigh," announced Burgess, with awful dignity, "is in the garden with Miss Lucy. Shall I inform her ladyship that Lord Deverell has arrived?"

"Whatever," said Maria, with a sigh.

Unperturbed by Burgess's dignified disapproval, the viscount plunked himself down, uninvited, in a nearby chair. As soon as the butler had departed, he said, "You might show a little interest, Maria. You haven't seen me in twenty-seven years."

"Well, of course I haven't, Harry. One doesn't *expect* to see a dead person. Unless one has a morbid turn of mind. Which I have not." And Mrs Latham fell to examining the diamonds on her fingers.

"Well, I'm not dead anymore," the viscount remarked, tapping his foot impatiently.

"No, you're not" was the unhelpful reply.

"In fact, I never was."

Another sigh. "How was I to know?"

Moments ticked by as the star-crossed lovers meditated. Then:

"Maria?"

"Yes."

"I missed you horribly."

"Well, I hope so, Harry," replied the lady. She considered for a minute, then raised herself to a sitting position and let her glance travel from the tips of his polished boots to his tanned face and his fair hair, so sun-bleached that it was impossible to be certain where the gold left off and the silver began. "I have missed you rather horribly myself." And for no apparent reason at all, she laughed.

The viscount sprang from his seat to take his long-lost bride in his arms.

"Why, Harry," she murmured as his lips met hers.

"Mama!" Isabella cried as she entered the room, to find her mother in the embrace of a stranger. It was quite the most shocking thing she'd ever seen; although her mother appeared to be participating most enthusiastically, and the stranger was, it must be confessed, a very handsome fellow.

Languidly, Maria drew away from Lord Deverell. "Ah, there you are, my love. What an unconscionable time you've been returning. Say hello to your papa, my dear."

EPILOGUE

Lord Hartleigh gently assisted his rather bulky wife into a comfortable chair on the terrace. Although he had, at the beginning, shown a rather alarming tendency to overprotectiveness, Isabella—with some help from her mother—managed to reassure the anxious father-to-be. He was at length convinced that it was not in his wife's best interest to be confined to her bed for nine months. After ascertaining that the walk from the garden had not caused her any irrevocable damage, he told her that she had a letter from his cousin.

"From Basil. Oh, thank heaven. I was so worried."

"I don't see why. Between his talent for gathering gossip and Henry Latham's talent for making money with it, he promises to do quite well for himself. Better than he deserves," the earl muttered, irritated anew as he remembered the trouble his cousin had caused him.

"Now, darling, he did write a very penitent letter before he left—"

"Maudlin, rather," the earl grumbled. But his wife reached for his cravat and pulled his head down so that she could plant a kiss on his forehead, and he remembered to be grateful to Basil for unintentionally thwarting those early plans to marry the fair Honoria. "Well then, let us see what he has to say."

" 'My darling Isabella,' " the countess read aloud.

"Not a promising start, the insinuating wretch."

" 'You will perhaps be pleased to hear that I have not

contracted any of the five hundred and eighty different varieties of foul disease that flourish in this abominable climate. That is because I am dying of a broken heart and haven't the strength to contract them.' "

"Broken heart, my foot."

" 'Nonetheless, even in my weakened state I have managed to be of some use to your uncle, who confesses himself astonished at the amount of helpful gossip I am able to relay to him. He informs me that my debt to him is now paid, and that whatever else I accomplish from now on is shared profit, my share being available to me for whatever wanton purposes I wish to pursue.

" 'Unfortunately, between the heat and the unending din of this vile city, I haven't the energy even to imagine any wanton purposes, nor would I have the strength to pursue such, could I imagine them. Therefore I am making a gift to your firstborn, care of your uncle, so that he or she might have at least one kind memory of the villainous Uncle Basil.

" 'Your uncle now talks of Greece, and suggests we might find something to our advantage there. No climate can be as vile as this one, and in the hopes that I might be set upon by marauding Turks, I have commenced packing my few miserable belongings, preparatory to leaving in the next week.

" 'Pray give my regards to my fortunate cousin, and you might pat Lucy on the head for me—if she'll stand for it. And if you can find it in your heart to forgive me . . . well, pray for me, Isabella—for I did love you as well as I could.

" 'Ever your affectionate and *humble* servant, B.' "

" 'Loved you as well as he could.' Well enough to spend your money and ruin your life—"

"He was desperate," Isabella reminded gently.

"And I was such a fool that without his interference, I wouldn't have realised how desperately in love with you I was."

"Was?" Isabella asked, tugging on his neckcloth again.

"Am. Will be. Always," Lord Hartleigh replied as he

dropped to one knee to gaze lovingly into the intelligent blue eyes of his countess. "From the very first day I saw you and you scolded me."

His wife gave a low chuckle of satisfaction, and pulled him closer for a kiss.

"Poor Basil," the earl murmured a few minutes later. "I wonder what will become of him?"

"Something dramatic, no doubt" was the whispered reply. The letter slipped from her lap to the floor of the terrace, was picked up by a breeze, and slowly fluttered, forgotten, to the garden.

If you have enjoyed this book and would like to receive details of other Walker Regency romances, please write to:

Regency Editor
Walker and Company
720 Fifth Avenue
New York, NY 10019